Into the War

Into the War

Translated by MARTIN MCLAUGHLIN

Mariner Books

Houghton Mifflin Harcourt

BOSTON · NEW YORK

First U.S. edition

www.hmhco.com

First published in Italy as *L'entrata in guerra* by Einaudi, Turin, 1954

This translation first published in the United Kingdom by Penguin Classics, 2011

Library of Congress Cataloging-in-Publication Data
Calvino, Italo.
[Entrata in guerra. English]
Into the war / Italo Calvino; Translated by Martin McLaughlin. —
First U.S. Edition.
pages cm.
ISBN 978-0-544-14638-9 (pbk.)
I. McLaughlin, M. L. (Martin L.) translator. II. Title.
PQ4809.A45E513 2014
853'.914—dc23   2014001374

Printed in the United States of America
DOC 10 9 8 7 6 5 4 3 2 1

Contents

Translator's Introduction

Italo Calvino (1923–85) spent the first twenty-three years of his life in San Remo, a provincial town in Liguria, near the French border. His date of birth (15 October 1923) meant he was just sixteen when Italy declared war, in June 1940, so his entry into adulthood also corresponded with Italy's entry into war (though he would only actually see combat when he joined the partisans in 1944).

As well as his date of birth, the place where he grew up also conditioned his life and outlook: he shared with his fellow-Ligurians a tendency to divulge little about himself; and he publicly claimed to be very wary of autobiographical writings, which he regarded as self-indulgent. Nevertheless, many elements in his fiction had a basis in the events of his life, and Calvino also wrote short autobiographical pieces at curiously regular nine-year intervals: this autobiographical trilogy, *Into the War* (in Italian, *L'entrata in guerra*, written 1952–53), was followed by two shorter pieces, *The Road to San Giovanni* (1962) and *From the Opaque* (1971).* The most substantial of these

---

* These two later works can be read in English in *The Road to San Giovanni*, by Italo Calvino, translated by Tim Parks (Jonathan Cape, 1993).

personal works was *Into the War*, a trilogy of short stories mixing memory and fiction, which first came out in book form in Italian in 1954. The present edition marks the first time that the trilogy has been published in English in book form. It is a brief classic on adolescence, on that liminal age before adulthood, which so fascinated Calvino because of its metamorphic potential and the different adult outcomes that could emerge from it.

In the author's own case (as in the case of all those of his generation in Europe), adolescence was perhaps a more crucial time than in other eras, as it was bound up with the major upheavals of world history, and, for Calvino, would eventually involve a perilous choice a few years later: the choice between joining up as a conscript in Mussolini's Fascist Republic or taking to the hills as a partisan. The reader here, in *Into the War*, encounters a different Calvino; one that is not the writer of the fantasy trilogy *Our Ancestors* (1960) nor the postmodern, self-reflexive author of *Invisible Cities* (1972) and *If on a Winter's Night a Traveller* (1979). This is Calvino the sharp-eyed realist writer, evoking his own landscape and his own past, never in an idyllic manner, but with a mixture of seriousness, comedy and, at times, poetry.

Although, in public, Calvino dismissed autobiographical fiction, or what he called 'the literature of memory', as rather decadent, the motivation behind these three stories is closely bound up with both the writer himself and his parents. The first story to be written, 'The Avanguardisti in Menton', was composed between 25 December 1952 and 18 January 1953, while the other two were written in the summer of 1953.

Calvino's father had died on 25 October 1951, so what ultimately became an autobiographical trilogy about a young man's entry into war and into life actually began as an homage to his recently dead father, exactly two months after the first anniversary of his death. In the end, the author's father only appears fleetingly in all three stories, and yet the whole trilogy finishes with an affectionate portrait of him, rising early in the morning and going up the country track with the dog to his farm at San Giovanni. It can also be argued that the last page of *Into the War* leads directly into Calvino's next autobiographical venture, *The Road to San Giovanni*, which was begun around the tenth anniversary of Mario Calvino's death, and which expands that final page into a more detailed description of that walk into the countryside above San Remo.

Throughout his life, Calvino had always felt distant from his father, who seemed to him out of touch with the times, like someone who belonged more to the nineteenth century, and so the figure portrayed in *Into the War* is clearly a realistic version of what later became Cosimo's exaggeratedly eccentric father in *The Baron in the Trees* (1957). In the title story, the father figure is seen as remote from what is happening in Europe, and, in the second tale, we see him and the author's mother obsessively trying to save rare species of plants while thousands of human beings are being slaughtered – 'mown down like hay', as Calvino's appropriately agricultural simile puts it. Yet, despite this distance, the final page of the last story adumbrates a rapprochement between father and son, a moment of closure that stresses the opposite notion to distance, the idea of the son's closeness to his unaware father: indeed the last word in the Italian original is 'vicino' ('close'). Although this trilogy is very much about a crucial stage in the young protagonist's life, there is also a strong thematic emphasis in the stories on the relationships between the different generations caught up in the war, including the protagonist's rapport with his parents, who appear at key moments in all three tales (i.e. near the beginning or end of each story).

However, partly because of its slightly emotional finale, Calvino felt dissatisfied with the trilogy *Into the War*. Immediately after completing it he wrote to his literary mentor, Elio Vittorini, telling him he had no desire to write other such tales; just after the book was published he told one reviewer that it was 'a dignified little book but not really essential'; and to another he said he was satisfied but also bewildered at its positive reception, since such works, he felt, prompt the crucial question: 'Once you start on the road to autobiography, where do you stop?' He regarded these three stories as a 'concession to autobiography', and his uneasiness about it culminated in 1968 when, in a letter to Guido Fink, he explained that he had turned to the memorialistic mode of *Into the War* under the influence of Giorgio Bassani, author of *The Garden of the Finzi-Contini*, but that he considers this turn an involution, and so is genuinely disappointed that Fink both remembers these stories so well and that he has actually quoted them twice. Therefore, given the author's lack of enthusiasm for the book, it is unsurprising that the trilogy was only reprinted once in his lifetime, in 1974.

Even though Calvino may not have started out with the idea of an autobiographical trilogy, these three tales have a striking unity in terms of themes, time and place. To reiterate, for Calvino, the entry into adulthood was contemporaneous with Italy's and his own entry into war. However, given the narrator's pre-military age, the war plays an important but largely background role in these stories. Mussolini, soldiers, sailors and air raids make only fleeting appearances, almost as 'walk-on parts', most notably at the end of the first story, when the narrator barely catches a glimpse of il Duce as he whizzes by in a car towards the front line. More emphasis is given instead to two elements of the narrator's increasing maturity: his growing awareness of social class and his developing ethical sense (it must be noted that, in 1953, Calvino was still a full member of the Italian Communist Party, whose ranks he had joined as a partisan).

The first of these elements, his sensitivity to the deprived and underpaid, surfaces in all three tales. In the first, 'Into the War', there is an initial contrast between the aristocratic Ostero and the protagonist, but, after this, the rural poor of what Calvino calls elsewhere 'the hidden face of Italy' dominate the story, which is set entirely in the school where they are temporarily housed. Similarly, the protagonist's tour of Menton in the second story, 'The Avanguardisti in Menton', begins in the rich villas overlooking the sea, but the real sense of the pity of war only emerges in the narrator's visit to the artisan's ruined shed in the older area of the town, while his rejection of the Fascist Captain Bizantini's attack on the proletarian sailors stems from the ethic inculcated in him by his parents, namely to oppose those who despise the poor and working people. Then, in the last piece, 'UNPA Nights', when the narrator and Biancone arrive in the old town, they at first consort with prostitutes and pimps, but their pranks and joking are silenced by their feelings of sympathy for the honest working-class people, who lie asleep and vulnerable in their run-down houses; and the penultimate scene at the harbour contrasts the fishermen setting out before dawn with the soldiers in the armoured column, who have halted momentarily to stretch their legs in the town.

In addition to awareness of social class, the protagonist's growing consciousness of morality and ethics is present in all three of the tales too. Early in 'Into the War' we hear about the influence of his parents' moral code on the protagonist, but the narrator takes care not to present too facile a story of ethical growth, so he says he is torn between morality and its opposite attitude, cynicism, and so ends up 'yielding' to a morality that is not without 'a veneer of cynicism'. In 'The Avanguardisti in Menton', his critical attitude towards the young Fascist commander in his fancy uniform is compared to the moralism that regular troops feel towards shirkers and bullies. In 'UNPA Nights', the narrator implicitly condemns the black-shirts, saying that their vulgar chorus betrays their true nature as 'soldiers of fortune, enemies of everyone and totally above the law'. Part of this ethical stance is dictated by the narrator's love for all things English (Calvino himself was a great Anglophile): in the first tale he alludes to the famous quote from *Hamlet*, as he realizes, when helping the sick, 'how many more things there are on earth, Ostero, than were dreamt of in our calm Anglophilia'. Similarly, in the second story, much of the action in Menton takes place in the town's former English club; and the last tale begins with the narrator arriving at the school with his magazine, showing pictures of English cities being bombed (this story is set in September 1940), but not really understanding the images – this last story ends with the protagonist going back to the magazine just after the enemy plane has flown over, now realizing the reality of air raids. The centrality of the author's concern with ethics here is also confirmed by what he says in an unpublished note on the trilogy, which follows at the end of this introduction. There Calvino states, in relation to this tripartite work, how he was primarily interested in portraying 'the work of the conscience, its hard-fought moral advances in adolescence'.

One of the most interesting aspects of this theme of ethical maturation is the way it relates to the different generations, especially in the first story. There we find not only the adolescent narrator, but also the child, who is the first victim of the war, scalded by boiling water in the power-cut; the old man, with whom the narrator establishes a bond; and the retired Fascist major. But, at the end, the real child turns out to be Mussolini, for whom war seems to be a kind of game, while the Italian people indulge him, like parents who are too kind to spoil his party. There is also a strong emphasis throughout the trilogy on the morality of the protagonist's parents. In the first two stories we are told at an early stage how outraged they were at the destruction wrought by the war, at the treatment of the poor Ligurian farmers, and at the behaviour of Italian troops in their houses. Unusually, there is no mention of the parents early in the final tale, but instead we find, in the last two paragraphs of the story, the aforementioned portrait of the protagonist's father getting up before dawn to go into the countryside to work, and implicit in this portrait is the father's work ethic and devotion to the land. This emphasis on morality and the older generations confirms once more the key role played by Mario Calvino's death in the genesis of *Into the War*.

Nevertheless, despite this mature-minded concern with class, morality, and opposition to Fascism, the adolescent narrator does not grow into a full adult in the course of the trilogy. Rather, a sense of failed initiation hangs over everything, a sense of thresholds not crossed, of doors not opened (literally so, in the second story, when the protagonist steals the keys and explicitly wonders about their symbolic meaning): it is certainly not a triumphant narrative of maturity. Sex appears in all three tales, but it is the protagonist's older friends who have sexual experiences, not the narrator himself, and, even in the last story, he lets Biancone go first with the prostitute and then loses interest. In each tale the narrator is morally rather ambiguous and aboulic, caught between an ethical stance and youthful cynicism, at times almost admiring the Fascists' exploits.

In fact, the dominant tone throughout, right from the start, is one of anticlimax. The English reader might compare this with the similarly ironic, downbeat tone in Evelyn Waugh's war trilogy, *The Sword of Honour*, begun around the same time, in 1952. For the protagonist of the first tale, 'Into the War', his front-line experience is deeply anticlimactic, since, in reality, it consists in merely helping the aged and infirm to eat and go to the toilet, and then, even at the end, the appearance of Mussolini in the car is largely missed by everyone: the tale had begun with il Duce declaring war and yet ends with him speeding by almost unnoticed. This sense of let-down continues in the other two stories: the long-awaited Spanish Falangists finally arrive, but barely notice the Italian Avanguardisti at the far end of the piazza; and, in the last tale, the protagonist and his friend spend a night *not* guarding the school, in case of air raids, and then the one plane that does fly overhead, at dawn, does no harm at all.

And yet, this final story, 'UNPA Nights', does more than just develop the feeling of anticlimax. It is perhaps the most complex of the three tales, in its mixture of narrative styles: a light-hearted portrayal of youth is combined with almost poetic descriptions of night-time in a blacked-out town. The comic tone is more prevalent than the poetic at first: Biancone, that characteristic figure, the more grown-up of the two schoolfriends, plays tricks on everyone – first on the narrator himself, then on the school caretaker, on the schoolteacher, on passers-by. There are wonderful moments of adolescent slapstick here, such as when the two boys perform a gas-masked version of La Lupescu's love affair with King Carol of Romania. The comedy is enhanced also by Calvino's deployment of another narrative code, that of the fairy tale: the elderly caretaker is portrayed as a witch, as she moves slowly along with her torch, while bats and moths fly round her and toads scamper from beneath her feet, so, when they arrive at the city boundary, the narrator fears she will mount on a broomstick and fly over the town.

The poetic tone emerges later, in some of the nocturnal descriptions. Night is a strong theme in all three tales, but the last story, set entirely in the hours of darkness, is almost a hymn to night, in which the narrator wants to wrap himself. It is also a nocturnal tour of San Remo: from the countryside, where the caretaker lives, to the old town, with its piazzas and brothels, right down to the harbour and the seawall, just before dawn. There is an increasingly poetic tenor to the descriptions of night here, particularly in the epiphanic scene at the end, where the narrator first watches the column of armoured cars halt, with their headlights blazing, then sits on the harbour wall near the prison, contemplating the town and watching the fishermen set out on their pre-dawn fishing expedition. This nocturnal emphasis is partly due to the fact that the terror of living in a city during a war is at its most acute at night-time, particularly during blackouts, which are mentioned on several occasions. But there is also, perhaps, an autobiographical motive behind these nocturnal evocations, particularly the scene at the harbour: Calvino, after all, had been imprisoned in the old harbour gaol in San Remo, and was lucky to make a narrow escape when the Germans were taking its prisoners off to Genoa.

This final story is also effective in bringing the trilogy full circle: the primary school was the scene of the serious help given by the protagonist to the aged and infirm in the first story, but here it is the scene of a final and largely comic tale. Similarly, an air raid which had indirectly caused a child's death is mentioned at the start of the first story, and another (in the end harmless) air alarm occurs at the end of the final piece, yet here the false alarm is contrasted with the photographs of the real bombing of English cities in 1940. Lastly, the role played by the protagonist's parents in the stories is rounded off by the paternal portrait on the last page: if the previous two stories had ended with the anti-climactic appearance of first Mussolini and then the Falangists, this tale, and the whole trilogy of war, ends with an almost pastoral portrait of the narrator's father arriving in the countryside in the early morning, just as the colours of the vines and olive trees start to emerge from the dark and the first birds begin to sing. From Homeric times the country landscape has been used as a counterpoint to scenes of battle, and here the emergence of colour and birdsong at the close of this war-time trilogy suggests a glimmer of optimism, perhaps the optimism that helped young anti-Fascists, like Calvino, who, thanks to his parents' moral code, made what he later considered to be the correct ethical choices in the dark days and nights of the Second World War.

Martin McLaughlin, 2011

An Unpublished Note by Calvino *on* Into the War

This book deals both with a transition from adolescence into youth and with a move from peace to war: as for very many other people, for the protagonist of this book 'entry into life' and 'entry into war' coincide. Here the war is something that people know little of as yet: the setting is the first period of Italy's intervention in what would become known as the Second World War; and the protagonist is a boy who is privileged in many respects, untouched by the trauma of more pressing problems, and who – perhaps for this very reason – still knows little about himself. However, the facts narrated already contain a large part of the future, prefigured and implied; and already there is at work in those facts, in their stop-start rhythm, the eternal interaction between the movement of collective history and the maturing of individual consciences. What I wanted to represent here was precisely the work of the conscience, its hard-fought moral advances in adolescence; and all this perhaps with an implied polemic against the more habitual image of adolescence in literature today.

This might have been the theme for a novel, had it not been for the necessity felt by us contemporary writers – whether this is a method or a limitation – to write by isolating a particular aspect in order to study it down to its core. In this way the book gradually structured itself into three separate pieces of narrative, which have in common the protagonist, the period and the place, as well as more or less the same mixture of memory and imagination, but each of them has an autonomous development and is modulated according to its own state of mind and its own rhythm. One cannot – as is well known – transform such tales into a novel simply by placing them alongside each other. For that reason, instead of following the chronological order of the facts narrated, it has been decided to leave the three stories [in the 1954 edition] in the order in which they were written, which is also the order in which the artistic thrust of each is best placed: the most evocative, bold and sincere story first ['The Avanguardisti in Menton'], the most compassionate and moralistic one next ['Into the War'], and lastly the one that is most compromised by elements of fun and emotion ['UNPA Nights'].

The book can also be considered – to use an image from war that is appropriate to the subject-matter – as an incursion that the author has carried out into the territory of 'the literature of memory', which is to him basically foreign territory. The raid was carried out in order to pit himself – like an enemy who does not fear hand-to-hand combat – against autobiographical lyricism, and to seek out in that land, too, the paths towards that narrative of morality and adventure which is dear to his heart. Just like anyone who carries out incursions, he hopes to come back laden with booty, and not to enrich his enemy with his own spoils.

Italo Calvino, *c.* 1954

A Note on the Text

The note on the previous pages was probably written around the time of the first publication of the trilogy, in 1954, and the reader will notice that in that edition the order of the stories reflected the chronological order of their composition: first 'The Avanguardisti in Menton', second 'Into the War', third 'UNPA Nights'.*

As for the text, Calvino's discomfort at writing this auto-biographical material is evident in the substantial cuts that he made in this trilogy between this first publication as a single volume in 1954 and the slightly shorter version printed in his collected short stories (*Racconti*, published by Einaudi in 1958), where the order of the stories reflects the chronological order of the facts narrated in them: the latter is the definitive version, found in the 1974 and subsequent editions, and the one on which this translation is based. In the 1958 *Racconti*, the three tales appeared in the section significantly entitled 'Difficult Memories'. In the first tale to be written, 'The Avanguardisti in Menton', he made no fewer than ten

---

* Calvino's note was found amongst his papers and published posthumously in his collected *Romanzi e racconti*, ed. Claudio Milanini, Mario Barenghi, Bruno Falcetto, 3 vols (Milan: Mondadori, 1991–94), I, 316–7.

major cuts over the first twenty-two pages of what is a twenty-five page story in the original Italian. Perhaps this was because it was the author's first full-scale autobiographical tale, and, in this first venture into 'the literature of memory', Calvino felt he was initially too expansive about close friends. Two of these major deletions were lengthy descriptions of his best friend, Biancone (his real name was Duilio Cossu); two gave more details about the enthusiastic Fascist schoolboy Ceretti; and he also excised other passages describing individual characters: Captain Bizantini, the Tuscan Federal Commander, a cartoon-like anecdote about the Fascist leaders Starace and Bottai, and a passage on the protagonist's own pessimism about the outcome of the war.

In the second tale written, the title story 'Into the War', nine passages were altered for the 1958 version, but these occur only over the first four pages of a fourteen-page story, most of them concerning his aristocratic friend, here called Jerry Ostero (in real life Percivalle Roero di Monticello), and Ostero's brother, who was killed at Tobruk. He also cut a couple of allusions to his father and the fact that he had left the rich tobacco fields of Yucatán to come back to Mussolini's Italy, as though it were a promised land.

Since, in the final tale, 'UNPA Nights', Calvino felt the need to excise just one passage about a peripheral character (the night-bird Palladiani), it seems as if he had gradually adapted to this autobiographical mode, i.e. not writing too many details about family and friends that he would later have to eliminate. However, the fact that, in the midst of this pruning of excessively personal memoirs, he retained the long closing passage describing his father reinforces its significance for the author as an act of literary *pietas*, making it a sequence that he was keen to retain, a literary settling of his debt to Mario Calvino.

★

The translator wishes to thank the following people for their expertise in helping solve a number of problems: Luca Baranelli, Mario Barenghi, Guido Bonsaver, Sarah Chalfant, Esther Calvino, Cathy McLaughlin, Mairi McLaughlin, Elisabetta Tarantino.

Martin McLaughlin, 2011

Into the War

The 10th June 1940 was a cloudy day. It was a time in our lives when we weren't interested in anything. We went to the beach in the morning all the same, myself and a friend of mine called Jerry Ostero. We knew that Mussolini was to speak in the afternoon, but it was not clear whether we would be going to war or not. On the sand nearly all the beach umbrellas were closed; we walked along the shore exchanging predictions and opinions, with sentences left trailing, and long silent pauses.

A bit of sun came out and we went on a catamaran, just the two of us and a girl with blondish hair and a long neck who was meant to flirt with Ostero, but in fact did not flirt at all. The girl was Fascist in her opinions, and normally would counter our talk with a lazy, slightly scandalized hauteur, as though dealing with opinions which were not even worthwhile refuting. But that day she was uncertain and vulnerable: she was just about to leave, and she did not want to. Her father, an edgy man, wanted to remove his family from the front before the war broke out, and had already rented a house in a little village in Emilia Romagna from September. That morning we continued to say how good it would be if we did not go to war, so we could relax and go swimming. Even the girl, with her neck craned forward and her hands between her knees, ended up by admitting: 'Oh yes . . . oh yes . . .' and then in order to dismiss such thoughts: 'Well, let's hope that this time, too, it's a false alarm . . .'

We came across a jellyfish floating on the surface of the sea; Ostero went over it with the boat so that it would appear beneath the girl's feet and frighten her. His trick did not work, because the girl did not notice the jellyfish, and simply said: 'Oh, what? Where?' Ostero showed off how coolly he could handle jellyfish: he brought it on board with his oar, and dropped it bellyside up. The girl squealed, but not much; Ostero flung the creature back into the water.

As we left the beach, Jerry caught up with me, quite full of himself. 'I kissed her,' he said. He had gone into her changing booth, demanding a farewell kiss; she did not want to, but, after a brief struggle, he had managed to kiss her on the mouth. 'I'm almost there now,' said Ostero. They had also agreed they would write to each other over the summer. I congratulated him. Ostero, who was easily excited about things, slapped me powerfully and painfully on the back.

When we saw each other again around 6 p.m., we were at war. It was still cloudy; the sea was grey. A line of soldiers was filing past, heading for the station. Someone applauded them from the terrace overlooking the promenade. None of the soldiers looked up.

I met Jerry with his officer brother, who was on leave and

in civvies, looking elegant and summery. He made a joke about how lucky he was, going on leave the day war was declared. Filiberto Ostero, Jerry's brother, was very tall, slim and bent slightly forward, like a bamboo stick, with a sarcastic smile on his blonde face. We sat on the terrace near the railway and he talked about the illogical way some of our fortifications near the border had been built, and about the mistakes made by headquarters in repositioning the artillery. The evening was drawing on; the thin outline of the young officer, curved like a comma, with his cigarette lit between his fingers without him ever bringing it to his lips, stood out against the cobweb of railway wires and the opaque sea. Now and again a train with cannons and troops on board would manoeuvre and then set off again for the border. Filiberto was unsure whether to give up his leave and go straight back to his company – driven also by the curiosity to check his glum tactical forecasts – or go to see a girlfriend in Merano. He and his brother discussed how many hours it would take to drive there. He was a bit afraid that the war would finish while he was still on leave; that would be quite funny, but harmful for his career. He got up to go to the casino to gamble; he would decide what to do depending on how his luck turned out. Actually, he said: depending on how much he won; in fact, he was always very lucky. And off he went with that sarcastic smile on his tense lips, the smile with which his image comes back to us even today, after his death in Tobruk.

The next day there was the first air raid alarm, in the morning. A French plane passed overhead and everyone stared up at it with their noses in the air. That night, another alarm; and a bomb fell and exploded near the casino. There was chaos around the gaming tables, women fainting. Everything was dark because the power station had cut electricity from the whole city, and the only lights to remain on above the green tables were the internal lights powered in-house, under the heavy lampshades which were still swinging to and fro because of the blast.

There were no victims, we discovered the next day, except a child in the old town, who, in the dark, had spilled a pan of boiling water over himself and had died. But the bomb had all of a sudden wakened and excited the city, and, as happens, the excitement focussed on a fantasy target: spies. All the talk was about windows seen lighting up and going dark at regular intervals during the alarm, or of mysterious characters lighting fires on the seashore, or even of human shadows in the open countryside making signals to aeroplanes by waving a pocket torch towards the starry sky.

Ostero and I went to see the bomb damage: the corner of a block of flats had collapsed, not much of a bomb really. People gathered round and made comments: everything was still within the parameters of things that were possible and predictable. There was a bombed-out house, but we were not yet inside the war, we did not know yet what it was.

However, I could not get out of my mind the death of that child scalded by the boiling water. It was an accident, nothing more: the child had bumped into the saucepan in the dark, a few yards from his mother. But the war gave a direction, a general sense to the idiotic irrevocability of that chance accident, which was only indirectly attributable to the hand that lowered the lever switching off the current at the power station, to the pilot whose plane buzzed invisibly in the sky, to the officer who had outlined his route, to Mussolini who had decided on war . . .

The city was constantly criss-crossed by armoured cars heading for the front, and by civilian cars full of evacuees with their goods and chattels tied onto the roof. At home I found my parents perturbed by the orders for immediate evacuation of our towns in the lower Alpine valleys. At the time my mother constantly compared the new war with the First World War, to imply that in this one there was none of the family trepidation and upheaval of emotions of the other one, and how the very same words – 'front' and 'trench' – sounded unrecognizable and strange. Now she remembered the exodus of refugees from the Veneto in 1917, and the different climate then, and also how this 'evacuation' of today sounded unjustifiable, simply imposed on people by a cold order from above.

As for my father's views on the war, he only said things that were beside the point, since he had lived in America for the first quarter of the century. He had always been someone who was out of place in Europe and out of touch with the times. Those mountains had been familiar to him from childhood days, and had been the setting for his exploits as an old hunter, but even that changeless landscape, he now saw, was in turmoil. He was anxious to know who was affected by the evacuation orders: which of his old hunting companions, people he knew in every remote village, and which of the poor farmers who constantly asked him for advice to appeal against taxes, and which of the greedy complainants whose disputes he was called upon to settle, walking for hours on end to establish irrigation rights for a thin strip of land. Now he could already see the abandoned terraces going back to seed, the dry walls crumbling, and the last families of wild boars – every autumn he would hunt them with his dogs – now leaving the woods, terrified by the cannon's roar.

For the evacuees, the newspapers proclaimed, the Fascist government and state assistance had prudently arranged board and lodging in villages in Tuscany, as well as transport services and refreshments, so that nobody should want for anything. In the primary school building in our town a shelter-point and human sorting office had been set up. All those who were enrolled in the Fascist Youth Movement were called up for service there, in uniform. Most of our school-friends were away, and so anyone could pretend not to have received the call-up. Ostero invited me to go with him to try out a new car his family had to buy after their own car had been requisitioned by the army. I said to him: 'What about the assembly?'

'Well, we're on holiday, so they can't suspend us from school.'

'But this is for the refugees . . .'

'And what can we do about them? They should be looked after by those who were always shouting "War, War!"'

But as far as I was concerned, this 'refugee' business held an appeal for me, though I could not have explained the reason for it precisely. Perhaps it was to do with my parents' sense of morality: my mother's civic morality, which stemmed from the first war and was both interventionist and pacifist at the same time, and my father's ethnic, local morality, his passion for those villages that had been neglected and oppressed. And as with the child scalded by boiling water, so now in the image of a lost crowd of people which the word 'refugee' conjured up in me I recognized a genuine, ancient fact, in which I was in some way involved. Certainly my imagination found more food for thought there than in the armoured cars, warships, aeroplanes, the illustrations in *Signal* magazine, all that other aspect of the war on which people's general attention was concentrated, as well as my friend Ostero's bitter technical irony.

Refugees were being offloaded from an old bus, by the school steps. I went along in my Avanguardista* uniform. At first glance, the sight of all those people clustered around and their shabby appearance, as though hospital-bound, made me as anxious as if I was arriving at the front line. Then I saw that the women, with their black kerchiefs on their heads, were the same ones I had always seen gathering olives and tending their goats, and that the men were the same as usual – our typically reserved farmers – and I felt I was in a more familiar environment, but at the same time an outsider, cut off. For the fact is that these people had made me feel uneasy even before. I was different from my father, and so it seemed like a reprimand if I watched them, say, saddling up

---

* Under Fascism, it was obligatory for school pupils to be in one of the Fascist youth organizations. Male pupils of pre-military age, from about fourteen to eighteen, were enrolled in the Avanguardisti. Younger pupils (eight to fourteen) were in the Balilla, a kind of Fascist Scout movement.

their mules, opening the furrows in a vineyard with their spades in order to water them, without ever being able to have a rapport with them, or even thinking of being able to help them. And they were still the same for me now, except they were a little more agitated, these people – the mothers and the fathers – intent on their worrying task of handing down the children from the bus, with their old folk sat on the steps, trying to keep the families close together and separate from the others. And what could I do for them? It was pointless thinking of helping them.

I went up the steps and had to go slowly, because in front of me on each step was an old lady, in black skirt and shawl, with her arms outstretched and her dry hands dotted with dark sores like diseased branches. Children were held in parents' arms in faded yellow bundles, out of which stuck heads that were as round as pumpkins. A woman who had been ill during the journey was vomiting, holding her forehead; her relations gathered around her motionless, staring at her. I felt no love for any of these people.

The school corridors had become encampments or hospital wards. The families had ended up against the walls, seated on benches, with their bundles and children, their sick relatives on stretchers, and those in charge trying to count up their own groups and never succeeding. Scattered and dispersed throughout these echoing halls one could see young Fascist Balilla Scouts, soldiers, officials in khaki uniform or in civilian clothes, but the only people in charge were, as far as one could make out, five or six Red Cross matrons, all sinewy and tense, as imperious as corporals, who manoeuvred that crowd of refugees and organizers and helpers as though they were on a parade ground, implementing a plan that was known to them alone. The order for the Avanguardisti to mobilize had not had much success, it seemed, not even among those who were always the first to put themselves on parade. I saw some of the corporals standing on their own, smoking. Two Avanguardisti were hitting each other and nearly crashed into a woman refugee. No one seemed to have anything to do. I had finished my tour of the corridor and had reached a door at the opposite end. By now I had seen everything and could go home.

On the far side the steps were deserted. The only thing there was a hamper, placed against a wall, on a landing half-way down the steps, and inside it was an old man. The basket was one of those long, low, wicker hampers, with two handles, to be carried by two people; it was leaning against the wall in an almost vertical position; the old man was crouching on the edge, which was on the ground, using the bottom of the basket as a back-rest. He was a small, stiff old man, paralysed, I would say, from the shapeless way he had crossed his legs; but the trembling which shook him would not let him stay still for a second, and made the hamper shake against the wall. He was toothless, and was muttering with his mouth open, staring straight in front of him, but not lethargic; on the contrary, he possessed a watchful, wild attention; he had an owlish look underneath the wing of a beret pressed down on his forehead.

I started down the steps and passed in front of him, crossing in front of the beam of those wide-open eyes. His hands could not have been paralysed: big and still full of force, they were gripped round the handle of a short knobbly stick.

I was about to go past him when his trembling became worse and his stammering more anxious; and those hands gripping the stick handle went up and down, striking the point of the stick on the ground. I stopped. The old man, tired as he was, beat the stick more slowly, and from his mouth emerged only a slow breath. I made to go away. He shook as though seized by hiccoughs, struck the ground, and started muttering again; and he got so agitated that the hamper bounced against the wall and started to topple. The big basket with the old man was about to tumble down the steps, had I not moved quickly to stop it. It was not easy to place it in a safe position, given its oval shape and the dead weight of the man inside, who was trembling but could not move an inch; and I had to have my hand constantly at the ready to hold the hamper if it slipped again. I was immobilized, too, like the paralytic old man, halfway down those deserted steps.

At last the steps filled with bustle. Two Red Cross people rushed up, in great agitation, and said to me: 'Come on, you as well, hold this here! Move, come on!' And all of us together lifted the hamper with the old man in it, and transported it swiftly up the flight of steps, all in a great hurry, as though we had been doing nothing else for the last hour and this was the final phase, and as if I was the only one showing signs of fatigue and laziness.

As I entered the crowded corridor, I lost them. Seeing me looking around, a militia group leader rushing by said: 'Hey, you, what time is this to turn up at assembly? Come here, we need you!' Turning to a man in civilian clothes, he said: 'Is it you, Major, who is a man short? You can have this chap here.'

Between two rows of straw mattresses, where poor women were removing their heavy shoes or were suckling babies, there was a round, pink gentleman, with a monocle, and hair that was parted very precisely and of a yellowish colour that looked as if it had been dyed or was a wig; his shoes had little white spats on top and the toecap was yellow and perforated with holes; on the sleeve of his black alpaca jacket he wore a blue strip, with the initials UNUCI.* This was Major Criscuolo, from the South of Italy, now retired, and a family acquaintance.

'Actually I don't need anyone,' said the Major. 'They're all already so well organized here. Ah, it's you?' he said, recognizing me, 'How is your mother? And the professor? Well, in any case, stay here, let's see.'

I stayed by his side; he smoked his cigarette through his cherry-wood cigarette-holder. He asked if I wanted a smoke; I said no.

'Here,' he said, shrugging his shoulders, 'there is nothing needing to be done.'

All around us the refugees were transforming the school-rooms into a labyrinth of streets like you would find in a poor village, unfolding sheets and tying them to ropes in order to get undressed, hammering nails into their shoes,

---

* The Unione Nazionale Ufficiali in Congedo d'Italia (UNUCI) is the Italian Reserve Officers' Association.

washing stockings and hanging them out to dry, taking fried zucchini flowers and stuffed tomatoes out of their bundles, and looking for each other, counting those in their party, losing and finding belongings.

But the dominant element in this sea of humanity, the intermittent but recurrent theme which first struck the eye – just as when entering a reception, the eye sees only the breasts and shoulders of the most décolleté women – was the presence in their midst of the lame, the village idiots with goitres, bearded women, female dwarves, people with lips and noses deformed by lupus, the defenceless look of those with delirium tremens. It was this dark face of the mountain villages that was now forced to reveal itself, to be put on parade: the old secret of the country families around whom the village houses huddle like the scales on a pine cone. Now, having been ousted from the darkness, they were trying to find some escape or some stability in the bureaucratic whiteness of that building.

In a classroom the old people were all seated on the benches; now a priest had also appeared and around him a small group of women was already forming; he was joking and trying to cheer them up, and a tremulous smile, like that of a hare, was forming also on their faces. But the more this semblance of country atmosphere took over their encampment, the more they felt somehow mutilated and dispersed.

'There's no doubt about it,' said Major Criscuolo, as he walked back and forwards with a nimble movement of his legs that never disturbed the crease of his white trousers, 'the organization is good. They all know their place, everything has been ordered in advance, now they'll dish out soup to everyone – a tasty soup, I've tried it myself. The rooms are big, well-aired, there is plenty of transport, and more on the way. Yes, of course, they are now off to Tuscany for a bit, but they'll have good lodgings there and be well nourished. The war won't last long, they'll see a bit of the world, some lovely towns in Tuscany, and then they'll come back home.'

The distribution of the soup was now the activity around which the whole life of the encampment revolved. The air was soft with steam and rang to the sound of spoons. Imposing and irritable, the supreme legislators of the community, the ladies of the Red Cross, were presiding over a steaming aluminium cauldron.

'You could go and hand out some bowls of soup,' the Major suggested to me, 'just to show you're doing something . . . '

The nurse who was holding the ladle filled me a bowl: 'Go towards the right, up as far as they've been served, and give this to the first one who hasn't had any.'

So, full of scepticism, I devoted myself to dishing out soup. I moved between two hedgerows of people, anxious not to spill soup and not to burn my fingers, but I felt that the little bit of hope I could instil in them with my bowlful was instantly lost amid the general bitterness and disapproval of their own condition, which, to a certain extent, I seemed to them to be responsible for; a bitterness and disapproval from which the comfort of a little drop of soup could certainly not distract them: on the contrary, it only served to accentuate those feelings, as it stirred up in them a well of basic desires.

I also saw the old man in the hamper again, leaning against a wall, in the midst of other luggage, resting stiffly on his stick, with his owlish eyes staring in front of him. I went past him without looking at him, as though afraid of falling under his spell again. I did not think he could recognize me in the midst of all that upheaval, but I heard his stick striking the ground, and him ranting.

Having no other way to celebrate our new encounter, I gave him the bowl of soup I was carrying, even though it was meant for someone else.

As soon as he took the spoon in his hand, a group of ladies from the regime's Social Assistance initiative came forward, with their black forage caps sitting at a jaunty angle on their curls, their black uniforms perkily stretched over their voluminous bosoms: one was fat with glasses, and another three were thin with make-up. Seeing the old man, they all said: 'Ah, here's the soup for old grandad! Oh, what lovely soup. And it's good soup, eh, it's good, isn't it?' They were holding in their hands some children's t-shirts, which they were distributing, and they held them out as though they wanted to try them for size on the old man. Behind them popped up other refugees, maybe daughters-in-law or daughters of the old man, and they stared diffidently at him eating, at those women and at me.

'Avanguardista, what are you doing? Hold his plate properly!' exclaimed the matron with glasses. 'Are you half-asleep?' In fact, I had become a bit distracted.

One of the daughters or daughters-in-law came unexpectedly to my defence: 'No, he can eat by himself, leave

him the bowl: he's got strong hands and can hold it on
his own!'

The Fascist ladies became interested: 'Oh, he can hold it
by himself! Clever grandad, look how well he holds it! There,
that's it, good man!'

I did not really have much confidence in leaving the bowl
solely to him, but the old man – whether it was the presence
of those women, or whether the soup aroused in him a nostal-
gia for lost happiness – got angry and yanked the plate out of
my hand, and would not let me touch it. And now we were
all standing there, myself and the ladies and the daughters-
in-law, our hands stretched out – the ladies holding their
t-shirts and little pyjamas – all surrounding the plate he was
holding as he trembled all over, the plate he did not want us
to have, and at the same time he continued eating and utter-
ing angry syllables and spilling soup on himself. Then those
silly women said: 'Oh, now grandad is going to give us the
bowl, isn't he, yes he's good at holding it himself (watch out!),
but now he's going to give us the plate so we can hold it for
him. Look out! It's falling, give it to us, for God's sake!'

All this attention only served to increase the old man's
anger, so much so that he dropped plate, spoon and soup,
dirtying himself and all around. We had to get him clean.
There were so many people bustling around and all of them
were giving me orders. Then someone had to take him to
the toilet. I was there. Should I run away? I stayed and helped.
When we put him back in the hamper, other doubts arose:
'But he's not moving this arm, not opening this eye! What's
wrong? What's wrong? We need a doctor . . .'

'A doctor? I'll go!' I said, and I was already running away. I went to the Major. He was smoking, looking out from a balcony, watching a peacock in a garden.

'Signor Criscuolo, there's an old man who's not well. I'm going to fetch a doctor.'

'Yes, good lad, that way you'll get out a bit. Look, if you want to come back even after half-an-hour, forty-five minutes, that's fine. In any case, everything's under control here . . .'

I ran to get a doctor and directed him towards the school. Outside it was one of those summery late afternoons when the sun no longer has any heat left in it but the sand is still burning and it is warmer in the water than in the fresh air. I thought about our detached attitude towards anything to do with the war, a detachment that Ostero and I had managed to take to an extreme level of coolness of style, to the point where we turned it into our second nature, a kind of carapace. For me now the war meant carrying paralyzed old men to the toilet, that was how far I had travelled: see how many more things there are on earth, Ostero, than were dreamt of in our calm Anglophilia. I went home, took off my uniform, put on my civvies, and went back to the refugees.

There I felt immediately at ease, light and agile. I was full of a desire to achieve things, I thought I could make myself genuinely useful, or at least make myself heard, be with other people. Of course, I had entertained the notion of disappearing, of going off to the beach, of stripping and stretching out on the sand, thinking about all the things that were happening in the world at that moment while I was lying there calm and idle. So I had toyed with the idea of being torn between

cynicism and moralism, as often happened to me, pretending
I was split between the two, and I had ended up yielding to
moralism, but not without retaining a veneer of cynicism.
All I wanted was to meet Ostero, in order to say to him: 'Hey,
I'm off to cheer up a few paralytics, a few scabby kids, you
coming?'

I instantly went to present myself to Major Criscuolo. 'Oh,
good lad, you're back: you were quick!' he said. 'All quiet on
the Western front here.'

As I was heading off, he called me back: 'I say, were you
not in uniform before?'

'I got it all stained with soup, helping that old man . . . I
had to go and change . . .'

'Ah, good man.'

Now I was ready to carry dishes, mattresses, accompany
people to the toilet. Instead I met a staff-sergeant, the one
who had assigned me to Criscuolo: 'Right, you, without the
uniform,' he called – fortunately he had already forgotten
that previously I had been wearing it – 'make yourself scarce;
the Federal Inspector is about to come, and we want him to
see only the right kind of people.'

I did not know where to go to make myself scarce. I
wandered amongst the refugees, torn between my fear or
disgust at ending up with the paralysed old man again and
the thought that he was the only one of all of them that I
had had some kind of dealings with, so my footsteps ended
up taking me back to where I had left him. He was no longer
there. Then I saw a circle of people looking down at the
ground in silence. The hamper was now placed on the

ground; the old man was no longer hunched up but laid out flat. The women were making the sign of the cross. He was dead.

That immediately posed the problem of where to take him, because the inspector was coming and everything had to be in order. A geometry classroom was opened up and permission was given to use it as a mortuary chapel. His relations lifted up the hamper and walked down the corridor; daughters, grandchildren and daughters-in-law followed after, some of them weeping. I brought up the rear, last of all.

Just as we were about to enter the classroom we met a group of young Fascist Party officials. They leaned over, their heads covered by their tall berets with the golden eagles, and looked into the hamper. 'Oh,' they exclaimed. The inspector came to offer his sympathy to the relations. He shook everyone's hand, one by one, shaking his head, until he came to me. He stretched out his hand to me as well, and said: 'I'm very sorry, yes, really very sorry.'

As evening fell, I headed home and it felt as if days and days had passed. All I had to do was close my eyes and I saw the long lines of refugees again, with their knobbly hands around the soup bowls. The war had that colour and that smell; it was a grey, swarming continent, in which we were now immersed, a kind of desolate China, infinite like the sea. Going back home was now like being a soldier on leave, who knows that everything he finds only lasts a short while, an illusion. It was a bright evening, the sky had turned reddish, and I was walking up a road between houses and pergolas.

Armoured cars went by towards the mountain road, towards the fortified roads at the border.

Suddenly there was a commotion, some people running along the pavements, getting caught in the string curtains at the fruit-sellers' and barbers' shops, and others saying: 'Yes, yes, it's him, look there, it's il Duce, it's il Duce.'

In an open-top car, beside some generals, and wearing the uniform of an army marshal, was Mussolini. He was going to inspect the front. He looked around and, since people were staring at him in astonishment, he raised his hand, smiled, and signalled that they could applaud him. But the car was going fast; he had disappeared.

I had barely seen him. What struck me was how young he was: a boy, he seemed, just a boy, as fit as a fiddle, with that shaved neck, his skin taut and tanned, his eyes flashing with anxious joy. The war was here, the war he had declared, and he was in a car with generals; he had a new uniform, his days were more active and hectic, he was crossing towns where he was recognized by people, in those summer evenings. And as though it were some sort of a game, he sought only the complicity of other people – not too much to ask – so much so that people were tempted to allow him it, in order not to spoil his party: in fact one almost felt a sting of remorse at knowing that we were more adult than he was, in not wanting to play his game.

The Avanguardisti in Menton

It was September 1940 and I was almost seventeen. After dinner I could not wait to go out again for a walk, even though I did practically nothing else all day but walk. Perhaps that was exactly the time when I began to enjoy living, even though I was not aware of it, because I was at the age when you are convinced that every new thing you gain is something you have always had. Because of the war, my own town's tourism had stopped and it had shrivelled, so to speak, into its provincial shell; I felt it was now more familiar and I could get the measure of it. The evenings were lovely, the blackout seemed an exciting new fashion, the war seemed something distant and routine: in June we had felt it looming over us, but just for a few astonishing days; then it seemed to be completely over; after that we stopped waiting. I was young enough to be able to live free of the alarm of being called up; and I felt I was outside that war both in terms of temperament and opinions. Yet each time I allowed myself to fantasize about my future I could not set it in any other context than the war: and then it was a war of derring-do, in which somehow I found myself happily free and different.

So I experienced both the pessimism and excitement of those times, and I lived in confusion, and went out to amuse myself.

I went into the piazza, and beside the Fascist Club I met some teachers who were looking for Avanguardisti to summon to an assembly, those with their uniform in order: they had to be there early the next morning. A trip to Menton was in the offing: a squadron of Young Falangists was due to arrive from Spain, and the Fascist Youth Movement of my home town had received the order to provide a guard of honour at the station in Menton: Menton had become Italy's new border post for the past few months.

Menton had been annexed to Italy, but it was still off-limits to civilians, and this was the first chance I had to visit it. So I put my name down on the list, along with that of my schoolfriend, Biancone, whom I promised to notify.

Biancone and I got on very well, even though we were both different types; we always liked to be present where new things were happening, and to comment on them from a position of critical detachment. However, Biancone was more inclined than me to get involved in the regime's initiatives and sometimes to imitate Fascist poses with a mimicry that bordered on caricature. Out of his love for a life full of action, he had gone to an Avanguardisti camp in Rome the year before, and had come back with the braid of a group leader. Something I would never have done, partly because of my innate incompatibility with leadership qualities, and partly out of my hatred for the city of Rome, where I had sworn I would never set foot as long as I lived.

The trip to Menton was a different matter: I was now curious to see that town, so near and so similar to my own, but which had become a conquered land, devastated and deserted; to be more precise, it was the only conquest we'd made during our war in June and was purely symbolic. We had recently seen a documentary in the cinema showing the battles fought by our troops in the streets of Menton, but we knew that it was all a charade, that Menton had not been conquered by anyone, just evacuated by the French at the time of France's collapse and subsequently occupied and ransacked by our boys.

For this undertaking Biancone was the ideal companion: on the one hand, he was, unlike me, close to people in the Fascist Youth movement; on the other, our school companionship had made us similar in tastes, in our language, in our sarcastic curiosity about events, and by going places together even the most tedious circumstances turned into a constant exercise in observation and humour. I would only go to Menton if he came too; that was why I immediately sought him out.

He was not in the usual billiard halls; to go to his house I had to go up into the old town. Under the dark archways lamps that were daubed with blue emitted a fake light, which did not reach the edges of the alleyways and cobbled steps, but was reflected only on the streaks of white paint marking the steps. I guessed I was passing by people sitting in the dark outside their houses, on their doorsteps or astride straw-bottomed chairs. The shadows were padded, so to speak, with these human presences, which manifested themselves in chatter, sudden calls and laughter, though always in hushed, intimate tones, and also sometimes in the white of a woman's arm or a dress.

From the darkness of an archway I finally popped out under the open sky: only then did I see, between the branches of a carob tree, that it was starless but clear. There the city finished its cluster of houses and started to dwindle into the countryside and to extend its untidy offshoots up the valleys. Beyond the walls of a garden the white shadows of the villas on the opposite slope let out only tiny slivers of light around the window frames. A road that was flanked by a metallic fence went halfway down the hill to the river, and there, in a little house topped by a terrace with a pergola, was where Biancone lived. In the calm air, filled with the sound of rustling reeds, I went closer, and whistled towards his house.

We met in the street, and Biancone was a bit surprised at my suggestion at first, because during that summer we had taken diligent care to avoid the Fascist Youth movement and its urgent attempts to enrol us for its 'Youth March', which seemed to epitomize the smug arrogance of that loud-mouthed institution. Now, however, the alarm was over, because the 'Youth March' was coming to an end, and in fact those Young Spanish Fascists were on their way to the final parade in front of Mussolini, in some city in the Veneto.

Biancone was immediately taken with my plan, and we talked excitedly about what we would do the next day, what would happen to our military conquests, and about the war. Of the latter we only knew the few things that had happened to our area during the days when it was just behind the front; and yet that was enough to give us the sense of the countries invaded by enemy armies. In June the order had come for immediate evacuation of the hinterland; we had seen the refugees passing through our town's streets, dragging carts laden with their meagre belongings: burst mattresses, bags of meal, a goat, a hen. The exodus did not last long, but long enough for them to find their homes and farms devastated on their return. My father had started to go around the countryside to take stock of the war damage: he would return home weary and saddened by the new losses he had calculated and estimated, but which, in his heart of hearts, in his parsimonious farmer's soul, were incalculable and pointless, like a human body that had been mutilated. There were vines that had been uprooted to supply posts for a billet, healthy olive trees cut down for firewood, citrus groves where mules tied to the trees had killed them off by gnawing away at the bark; but there was also – and here the outrage seemed to be turned against human nature itself, and was no longer the fruit of vulgar ignorance, but a warning about a latent, painful ferocity – vandalism inside houses: smashing everything, down to the last cup in the kitchen, into a thousand pieces, defacing family photographs, reducing beds to shreds, or – overcome by God knows what depraved perversity – shitting into plates and saucepans. On hearing such tales, my mother said she could not believe such things could have been done by our people; and we were unable to draw any other moral except this: that for the conquering soldier every land is enemy territory, even his own.

At times, some of these stories would plunge me into lonely rages, twisted frenzies that found no outlet. To recover from them I would turn, with the fickleness of inclination of the young, to cynicism: I would go out, meet friends I could trust, and I was calm, clear, sneering – 'Hey, have you heard the latest?' – and the things that had in private seemed to torment me now became quips, retorts full of paradoxical bravado, to be said with a wink, with a brief laugh, almost with approval and admiration for those exploits.

That was the kind of thing Biancone and I said as we talked quietly in the dark street outside his house, lowering our voices every so often almost to the point of not being able to understand each other and conversely ending up by saying the most outrageous things very loudly, as always happened to us. I did not know whether Fascism was also for Biancone something he had to suffer, or rather a joyous opportunity to share the two different natures, the two different privileges, of his character: the facility with which he assimilated himself to the Fascist style, and at the same time the critical acumen which our precocious vocation towards opposition had nurtured in us. Biancone was shorter than me, but stronger and more muscular, with a face that had haughty, square features, especially in his jaws, jawbones and the clear outline of his forehead; these features of his were contrasted with the pallor that set him apart from the young people here, especially in the summer. The fact is that in summer Biancone slept all day and went out at night: he did not like the sea nor life in the open; and his favourite sports were wrestling and exercises in the gym. His was a lined face, that of an old man; I thought I could read in it the bitter initiations of his nocturnal wanderings, which I thoroughly envied him.

But this face of his had a strange capacity to take on Mussolini's expressions: sticking out his lips, raising his chin, keeping his solid neck erect with its straight nape, and also stiffening into military poses when you least expected it; with these reflexes and his lapidary replies he often used to confound our teachers and get out of trouble. His most obvious characteristic was the way he combed his smooth, black hair: a strange style like a helmet or Roman ship's prow, divided by a very precise parting. It was a hairstyle invented by him and of which he was very fond.

We said goodbye, agreeing to meet at assembly time. Biancone went away to wind up his alarm. I went off to warn my parents to wake me. 'What are you going there for?' my father asked: he could see nothing interesting about an empty city.

My father and mother had a permit to allow them to go to Menton once a week: they had been entrusted with the care of some gardens full of rare and exotic plants, which were the property of enemy subjects. They came back with their sample-holders full of diseased leaves; their visits only served to verify the progress made by the insects, weeds and drought in the abandoned flower beds. The beds would really have needed gardeners, work, expenditure, whereas all they could do was to help a particular precious exemplar, to fight against a fungus, to save a species from extinction. They persisted in those gestures of vegetal *pietas* at a time when already whole peoples were dying, mown down like hay.

The next morning I went out early; it was grey; because of the time, I thought, but also because of the clouds. Beside the Fascist Club there were still only a few Avanguardisti, all boys I knew but who were not really my close friends. They were buying loaves of bread with ham in a café that had just opened and were biting into them and pushing each other in the middle of the road. More continued to arrive, one by one, not in any hurry: they saw there was still time and went off again with a friend to buy food or cigarettes. None of my friends were there. Most of them were boys who, in that semblance of military discipline as practised by the Fascist Youth, moved with an aggressive nonchalance, like pirates, whereas I could never be spontaneous and free.

The deadline for the assembly had passed some time ago; the Avanguardisti were gathering in large groups along the street, but there was no sign yet of either the bus, nor our leaders nor Biancone. I was used to my friend's late arrivals, which he always mysteriously managed to make coincide with the late arrivals of our superiors or with delays in the organization of ceremonies, perhaps because of that innate knack of his of identifying himself with those who told us what to do. But on this occasion I was really worried that he would not show up. I had approached some of the more reasonable and discreet types, but they were people I knew to be the least interesting: for instance, a certain Orazi, who was studying to be a technical engineer, and who looked around him with a calm, blue gaze, and spoke slowly about the short-wave radios he was building. Orazi would have been an excellent companion for the trip, but he had none of that spirit of discovery, that witty conversation that characterized Biancone's company. I knew that for the whole of the journey he would only drone on about his radios, and the sights that would capture his attention would be mechanical or architectural curiosities or things to do with ballistics, which he would explain in great detail. So the trip to Menton no longer held any attraction for me. The fact is, I still had that need for friends that is typical of the young, in other words: the need to give sense to what they live through by discussing it with others; what I mean is that I was far from that manly self-sufficiency that can only be acquired through love and which is a mixture of integration with others and solitude.

Suddenly I heard Biancone talking behind me: he was with the others, joking, and had already entered into the morning's spirit of mockery, as though he had always been there. As soon as Biancone arrived, everything took on another rhythm. The officers popped up, clapping their hands: 'Come on, come on, quickly now, are you all asleep?' The coach arrived, we started to form a queue and divide ourselves into groups. Biancone was one of the group leaders and was instantly told what his duties were. He called me with a wink into the squad he would command, and he jokingly threatened us with God knows how many laps of running as punishment for something or other. The window of the armoury opened and one by one each of us was quickly given a rifle and other accoutrements by a sleepy and irascible militia-man. We climbed on to the coach and set off.

We were going along the Riviera and the officers urged us into a song, which soon died out. The sky was still grey, the sea a glassy green. Near Ventimiglia we looked with curious eyes at the houses and cement ponds which had crumbled under the explosions: they were the first bombed-out homes we had seen in our lives. From the entrance to a railway tunnel the famous armoured train, Hitler's gift to Mussolini, was sticking out; they kept it under there to prevent it from being bombed.

We approached the old border at Ponte San Luigi, and Captain Bizantini, who was leading us, started to stir up national pride over this business of Italy's borders moving. But the conversation quickly dwindled into an embarrassed silence, because, in that initial period of the war, the topic of our Western borders was delicate and embarrassing even for the most avid Fascists. For our entry into the war at the moment when France collapsed had not taken us to Nice, but only to that modest little border town of Menton. The rest would come our way, they said, at the peace settlement, but by now the idea of a triumphal entry with full pomp had faded, and even in the hearts of those who had least doubts there was the worry that that disappointing delay might go on indefinitely; and the feeling spread that Italy's fate was not in Mussolini's hands but in those of his powerful ally.

By the time we got to Menton it was raining. The rain was coming down heavily in thin showers over the horizon-less sea and the villas that were all locked and bolted up. In the midst of the rain was the city sitting on its rocks. Military motorbikes ran across the shiny asphalt of the promenade. On the rain-streaked windows of the coach gleamed fragmentary images, and behind each one a whole world opened up for me to discover. In the tree-lined avenues I recognized the misty cities of the North I had never seen: was Menton Paris? There was an Art Nouveau shop-sign: was France the past? There was nobody to be seen except for the odd senti-nel sheltering in his garret, and builders using bags as rain hoods. And greyness, eucalyptus trees, and the oblique lines of field-telephone wires.

We got out; it was raining; it seemed that we were imme-diately to form ranks at the station, but instead we all got back on the bus again and went to another place – I don't know what it was: a villa that had been requisitioned, maybe – then a walk for a bit in the rain, up to a kind of smaller villa that was empty, which could also have been a school or a gendarmes' barracks, and there we left our rifles in a row, leaning against the wall, out of the rain.

Our clothes gave off a damp smell: I was quite happy, because my uniform had always kept its depressing, dusty smell of the depot, which maybe this time would go away. Nobody knew when those Spaniards were meant to arrive, as there was no timetable for the trains coming from France, so every so often a group leader would come back shouting: 'Assembly! Assembly with rifles!'; but then, again, we would hear: 'Dis-miss!' At times it seemed that no one in the whole of Menton had ever heard anything about the Spanish, at other times it was as if they were expected any minute; in fact, at one point they were arriving at 'ten past eleven', as we were assured by a rumour that continued to circulate until five past eleven, and then petered out.

We ate everything we had brought from home, standing up, under the little portico of the barracks-villa, watching the rain pouring onto the empty garden. Between one assembly and another some people had managed to find a way of escaping, going around the town and buying cigarettes and orangeade. It seemed that there were some shops open nearby, catering specifically for the builders.

At midday the sun came out and it stopped raining. They were unable to keep us there any longer and everybody headed off in small groups, so they gave us half an hour of leave. Biancone and I went off on our own, rejecting as too pathetic the pursuit of merely a tobacconist or a billiard hall, and as too unlikely the search for women. We walked slowly, looking at the French slogans which had been cancelled out, the timid signs of life from the few families who had been repatriated – shopkeepers, mostly – and broken windows, the houses which had been hit and which had a plastery, convalescent look. We ended up on a series of minor roads, halfway into the countryside. A builder from the Veneto told us that the new border was five minutes away and we hurried off in that direction. There was a valley with a stream, the Italian flag and, in the distance, the French flag. An Italian soldier asked us in hostile terms what we wanted, and we replied: 'Just looking.' And we looked, in silence. Over there was France, the defeated nation, and here Italy began, Italy which had always won and would always win.

As we returned late to the assembly point, some people were coming away and there was apparently good news: 'They're here! They're here!' 'Who? The Spanish?' 'No, the people bringing lunch.' Apparently a van had arrived with food for all of us. But nobody knew where it was: where we were there were neither officers nor assemblies. We continued roaming round the town.

In a bombed-out square covered with earth, a monument had survived: a female figure in a long skirt was bending down towards a young girl coming towards her; at the side of this scene was a cockerel. It was the monument to the 1860 plebiscite: the girl was Menton, and the woman was France. So our scepticism triumphed over easy targets: on the one hand, we mocked the Roman eagles on our uniforms, and on the other, that little scene out of a reading book; the whole world was stupid and only the two of us were witty and clever.

I could not bring to mind my memories of boyhood trips to France. Now Menton gave me the impression of a weary, monotonous town. Our column was going along the avenues, heading for the mess; the rumour was that the Spaniards were not coming until the next day and that we would have to spend the night there. I felt that I had seen the whole of Menton by now, and I felt disappointed by it. And I was fed up with that company and that mixture of relaxation and discipline that held us in its grip; I could not wait to get away. We passed by big grey Art Nouveau buildings all boarded up. What was missing were those insignificant details, like the colours of paint on the walls around shops or the different bodywork of their cars that give a sense of a life that was different from ours though very close to us: the sense of a France that was alive. This was a France that was dead, it was an Art Nouveau sarcophagus that the Avanguardisti were marching through, chanting 'The Roman Anthem', while the sight of a hotel's minarets and oriental domes, or the Pompeian-style decorations on a villa, gave it the feeling of a theatre with its lights out, with scenery discarded and in disrepair.

The mess began about five. A group of Young Fascist Sailors from *** * also arrived, a bunch of beanpoles, that we glared at as intruders. The Federal Commander had also come with them, and Bizantini presented our group. The Commander asked if the mess had been sufficient, and announced that we would be spending the night there. I was seized by a powerful sense of melancholy; my comrades raised cries of enthusiasm.

He was a young commander, from Tuscany. He wore a uniform of khaki gabardine, with cavalry twill trousers and yellow boots; but this outfit, military in appearance, was in its cut, material, lightness, and in the arrogance with which he wore it, the furthest thing you could imagine from the army's uniforms. And perhaps because of my awkwardness in the way I wore my uniform, because it had been forced on me, and because I was predestined to belong to those human beings who have uniforms imposed on them and not to those who use them as an instrument of authority or for pomp, I felt myself moved by the moralism, the always slightly envious moralism, of the regular troops against shirkers and bullies.

Some of the Avanguardisti from my home town, sons of small-time local leaders or functionaries, were old acquaint-

---

* In a number of stories, and so presumably also here, Calvino used three asterisks to denote his home town of San Remo (each asterisk probably corresponding to a syllable).

ances of the Commander, and he joked along with them; as far as I was concerned, this atmosphere of comradely complicity made me feel slightly uneasy, and I far preferred the flat peremptory tone that I had become used to accepting. I went to look for Biancone in the crowd, in order to comment on these events, or rather to collect and pick out together the details which we would talk about later at our ease. But Biancone was nowhere to be found; he had disappeared.

I came across him again at sunset while I was wandering along the seafront with its low, prickly palm trees. I was already gloomy. The slow beating of the sea against the rocks mingled with the natural stillness of the countryside and enclosed in a kind of circle the deserted city and its unnatural silence, which was broken now and again by isolated noises echoing through it: the ta-ra-ra of a trumpet, a song, the roar of a motorbike. Biancone came towards me making a great fuss, as if we had not seen each other for a year, and he told me the news that he had been picking up: a beautiful girl had apparently been sighted, in a grocer's store – she had been in a concentration camp in Marseilles – and now all the Avanguardisti were going there to buy a few lire's worth of goods just to see her; in another shop it seemed that French cigarettes could be bought, for almost nothing; in one street there was a broken, abandoned French cannon.

Biancone had a euphoric mood that was really too expansive for the insignificant news he had; and I had not forgiven him for having gone off without me. Continuing his discussion, he mentioned the scenes of devastation those houses must have witnessed in June, and incidentally, he said, yes, there were some houses that were wide open and you could go in and see everything that had been wrecked and scattered on the floor. But in his talk, which seemed to be rather generic, every now and then some very precise details stood out. 'But were you there too?' I asked. Yes, he had been there, he told me; going around with some of the other lads, he had gone into a couple of houses and hotels that had been destroyed. 'Pity you weren't there,' he said. His going away without me now seemed an unforgivable piece of treachery. But instead of showing I was hurt, I preferred to make an enthusiastic suggestion: 'But we could go back there together . . .?' He said it was now dark, and we would not be able to see where we were treading in the mess of those places.

When we were all together again in the dormitory (it had been hurriedly kitted out in a gym, with straw mattresses stretched out on the floor), the visit to the bombed-out houses was the topic of all general conversation. Everyone was talking about the extraordinary sights they had seen around the town and quoted names that seemed to be familiar to everyone else, such as 'at the Bristol', 'at that green house'. These explorations had seemed to me at first to be an experience restricted to that small circle of the most enterprising lads, who formed a band on their own; but gradually I saw others talking about their experiences, even guys like Orazi, who had initially remained aloof and just listened. My loss seemed to me to be irrecoverable: I had wasted that day in a grumpy mood, without even grazing the secret of the city, and the next day they would wake us early, line us up at the station for a couple of 'Present arms!', and then all back onto the coach again, and the vision of a looted town would disappear from my sight forever.

Biancone passed close to me, carrying a pile of blankets, and said in a whisper: 'Bergamini, Ceretti and Glauco have got swag.'

I had already noticed, in the midst of the mattresses, some commotion which I couldn't really understand: and now that Biancone had put me on the alert, I remembered having seen shortly before a tennis racquet being spun in Bergamini's hand, and wondering at the time where it had come from. Now I could no longer see the racquet, but just at that point Glauco Rastelli, who was folding down the blanket on his mattress, revealed a pair of boxing gloves, which he instantly hid beneath it again.

Biancone had already got in under the covers and was leaning on his elbow, smoking. I went over to sit on his mattress. 'We're in a good team,' I said.

'Oh yes,' he replied, 'a top gang, our fellow-henchmen!'

'We weren't like that when we were fifteen.'

'Ah, those were different days!' said Biancone.

Just then a 'Cuckoo! Cuckoo!' sound wheezed and whistled in the dorm; and Ceretti rolled over on his mattress in delight at having succeeded in making the cuckoo clock he was struggling with work.

'But how'll they ever get all this stuff home?' I asked Biancone. 'He can't hide a cuckoo-clock under his jerkin, can he?'

'He'll chuck it away. What do you expect him to do with it? He only took it to muck about with.'

'As long as he doesn't make it go cuckoo all night, and lets us sleep,' I replied.

'Hey, guys,' Ceretti himself then said, 'I've now wound it up; from now on it'll go off every half-hour.'

'Chuck it in the sea! Get rid of it!' And four or five of them, already without their boots, flung themselves onto his mattress, on top of him and his clock. They continued fighting until the clock was stopped.

Soon, once the lights had gone out, the carry-on also died down. I could not get to sleep. In a gym-hall adjoining ours were billeted the Young Fascist Marines from ***. We had not felt like fraternizing with them, possibly because they were older than us, or because of ancient rivalries between different parishes in the town, or perhaps more because of class differences, since they apparently belonged to a kind of harbour-area proletariat, whereas the majority of us were students. Even after the wildest of our lot had suddenly gone from making a racket to sleeping, these young sailors continued to raise merry hell, moving about and playing tricks on each other. They had a dialect call of their own, probably invented that same day in God knows what circumstances, and it was hugely funny for them, though mysterious to others: 'O bêu!', meaning, I think, 'Oh moo-cow!', a cry they emitted like a cow mooing, dwelling on that vowel that was half e and half u, perhaps mimicking a shepherd's call. One of them, lying down, would shout it out in a low voice, and all the others would roar with laughter. For a while it seemed that they had finally fallen asleep, and I was trying to grasp onto sleep myself, when another voice further away in the distance would start up again: 'O bêu!' And at the protests and threats which some of us shouted at them, they would reply with fresh waves of yells and cries. I wanted a group of us to march into their room and give them a doing, but the most belligerent amongst us, in other words Ceretti and his gang, were sleeping as if it was all quiet, and the insomniacs among us were too few and indecisive. Biancone was also amongst those who were sleeping.

Between my thoughts about my looting comrades and my irritation at that racket, I continued to toss and turn under the rough military blankets. In those days, an aloof resentment shaped many of my thoughts; and the way I considered and opposed anything to do with Fascism was also aloof. That night Fascism, the war and the vulgarity of my comrades were all of a piece for me, and I bundled everything up into the same feeling of disgust, and I felt I had to put up with everything without any hope of escape.

So I still looked at them with resentment, those young marines, when I saw them the next morning, filing by in the garden, thin, lanky youths, with a lazy step that was indifferent to orders, while Captain Bizantini inspected our arms as we lined up on parade.

When we protested about their behaviour the night before, Bizantini added his own recriminations; he shared our local animosity, out of hierarchical rivalry with those in the Young Fascist movement from the main town, and started to say:

'Yes, you see, a fine example of young sailors they've sent from ***! Do you call that youth? They're kids who've never done any sport: hunched over like hooks, gangly, look at their lop-sided shoulders!'

He was exaggerating, but he was not totally wrong. They certainly were not athletic types, but, to tell you the truth, neither was I, and in that sense I was on the same side as them against Bizantini's sarcasm.

'Tramps, harbour porters, navvies! They come here to pick up the few lire per day without working . . .' And the more he talked, the more I felt my recent anger against them subside, and in its place there resurfaced the morality in which I had been brought up, which was to oppose those who despise the poor and working people.

'With all the regime does for the people . . .' Bizantini went on.

The people . . ., I thought. Were these young sailors the people? Were the people well or in a bad way? Were the people Fascist? The people of Italy . . . And as for me, who was I?

'. . . they couldn't give a damn either about the Young Fascists or anything!'

'Nor me! Nor me!' I whispered to Biancone, who was standing beside me.

And Bizantini went on: 'Oh, but the Commander has taken it on board, he noticed it at once: that we've brought lads who are all students, all well turned out, solidly built, well-educated boys . . .'

'Bullshit,' I said in a whisper to Biancone, 'shit.'

'He said he would make sure we're prominently seen by these Spaniards . . . by the Caudillo's young men.'

The line of young sailors had disappeared; Bizantini was going on with his speech, while I followed my thoughts: maybe we would spend another day in Menton and I wanted Biancone to come with me to see the looted houses. 'As soon as he lets us go,' I said to him under my breath, 'let's go off together.' He, impassive even when standing at ease, gave me a wink.

The captain continued to spout out his philosophy, and was now comparing education in Mussolini's time with education in the past: 'The fact is that you have been brought up under Fascism and you don't realize what that means! For example, last night, here in Menton, if there had been some of those old teachers from days gone by, you have no idea what a fuss they'd have made: "For goodness' sake, they're just boys, how can you make them sleep outdoors, and there are no beds, and whose responsibility is it, and the families . . ." Ha! Fascism instead says: at the double, no problem, let's get on with it. Roman education, just like Sparta. No beds? Sleep on the ground, all soldiers together, for God's sake! Right turn: march!'

So the captain revealed himself for what he was, the most naïve of all of us: with a bunch of hairy boys and shirkers who could not wait to ransack a town, he got all emotional, like a grandmother, excited by the big adventure of making us spend a night away from home! And the rank and file of Avanguardisti responded to his 'One-two! One-two! N-two . . .' with raspberries, belches and farts.

Biancone had heard about a villa nearby: according to those who had been there, it was interesting, but he had not seen it yet. In its garden a finch was singing, and drops of water were falling in a pond. The grey leaves of a huge agave were covered with the names of people, cities, regiments, carved with bayonet-tips. We wandered around the villa, which seemed closed, but on a veranda with broken windows we found a French door that had been unhinged. We went into a sitting room with armchairs and sofas in disarray, covered in a shower of tiny bits of broken crockery. The first looters had searched for silverware in the cupboards and flung out the china dinner services; and they had pulled away the rugs from under the furniture which had stayed overturned, as though after an earthquake. We went through rooms and corridors that were dark or illuminated depending on whether the shutters were closed or open or, indeed, pulled off, constantly bumping into things that were sitting haphazardly on ledges or scattered on the ground and trampled: pipes, socks, cushions, playing cards, electric wire, magazines, chandeliers. As he proceeded, Biancone would point to every item, not missing a detail, connecting one thing with another, and he would bend down to pick up the stem of a broken glass, a strip of upholstery that had been torn off, as though he were taking me to see flowers in a greenhouse, and he would then put everything back where he had found it, with the light, careful hand of an inspector investigating the scene of a crime.

We climbed to the upper floors up a marble staircase that was filthy with footprints, and found rooms a-flutter with veils.

These were pyramid mosquito nets: there must have been one suspended over every bed; and the first looters had ripped them down and dragged them to the ground. Now all that tulle, with its drapes and flounces, covered the floors, beds and chests of drawers with a mantle of gauze that was puffed-up and twisted. Biancone enjoyed this vista very much, and he moved through the rooms parting the veils with two fingers.

In one of those bedrooms we heard a rustling sound: something like a big beast was kicking underneath the covering of tulle.

'Who goes there?'

'Who goes there?'

It was Duccio, an Avanguardista from our squadron, about thirteen years old, fat and squat and red in the face.

'There's a lot of stuff, have you seen?' he said, out of breath: he was going through a chest of drawers.

He took out things from the drawers. If they were no use to him, he chucked them on the floor; if they were of use, he stuck them in his hunting jacket: sock-suspenders, socks, ties, brushes, towels, a jar of brilliantine. Through cramming so much stuff into his jacket he had given himself an almost spherical hump, and he was still sticking scarves, gloves and braces under his jersey. He was swollen and puffed up front and back like a pigeon, and showed no sign of stopping.

We no longer paid him any attention: we had heard a quite distinct noise, as of someone hammering, echoing from the floor above. 'What can that be?'

'Nothing,' said Duccio, 'it's Fornazza.'

Following the sound, we reached the floor above, in a kind of attic, where our comrade Fornazza, who was as tall as Duccio, but was thin and dark-skinned, with thick curly hair, was attacking an old chest of drawers with a hammer and screwdriver.

'What are you doing?' we asked.

'I need these handles,' he said, and he showed what was in his hand. He had already unhinged two of them.

We left our comrades to their work and continued our tour of the villa. In the attic we went out through a skylight onto a small roof terrace. From there we had a view over the garden and the green area all around, and Menton, and the olive trees, and, in the distance, the sea. There were some rotting cushions and we placed them against the pole of the radio aerial, and we stretched out in the sun to smoke in peace.

The sky above was clear, with a few white wisps of cloud flying around the aerial like twisted flags. From below came the sound of voices amplified by the emptiness of the streets, and we recognized them. 'That's Ceretti on the hunt, the other one is Glauco getting angry.' Through the little columns on the balustrade we could see Avanguardisti and Young Fascists popping up all over the town: a group of them turning at a crossroads; two appearing somehow at a window of a house, sending out a whistle; and through one of the gaps we watched our officers emerging from a bar near the sea, all euphoric around the Commander. On the sea there were reflections of the sun's rays.

'So why don't we go for a bathe?'

'Coming?'

'Let's go.'

We ran downstairs, headed downhill and went to the beach. On the other side of the promenade, on a strip of sand and stones, a group of half-naked labourers were eating in the sunshine and passing around a bottle.

We stripped and stretched out on the beach. Biancone had white skin covered with moles, while I was dark-skinned and thin. The sand was dirty, full of seaweed shaped like dark, prickly bullets and rotting grey beards. Biancone could already see clouds approaching the sun, discouraging the idea of a swim, but I ran and dived in and he was forced to follow suit. The sun really did disappear and swimming in that water the colour of fish was a bit miserable, as was seeing above us the cliffs over the railway embankment and the silent town of Menton. A soldier with his rifle and helmet came out to the end of the pier and began to shout. He was shouting at us: it was a prohibited area, we had to come back to the shore. We swam back, dried ourselves, got dressed and headed for the mess.

We did not want to waste the afternoon in more distant, isolated villas, but wanted to stick to the town houses, where every landing opened up different worlds, every threshold the secrets of another life. The doors of flats had been forced and on the floors were scattered the contents of the drawers that had been overturned in the search for money or jewellery; and rummaging amid those layers of clothes, knick-knacks, papers, you could still find objects that were worth something. By now our comrades were working their way systematically through every house, grabbing anything decent that was left; we would meet them on the stairs, in corridors, and sometimes we would join up with them. It must be said, they never stooped to hunting for things, as we had seen Duccio do; when they found anything interesting or eye-catching, they would take it, flinging themselves on it with a shout before the others arrived; later maybe they would throw it away, if it got in the way or they found something better.

'And what have you found?' they asked us. I would growl between my teeth: 'Nothing', torn as I was between flaunting my disapproval and a residual feeling of childish embarrassment at being different. Biancone, on the other hand, waved his hands about, giving detailed explanations: 'Oh, you should see what we saw! We know a place! You know just at the bend? Well, that house that's been half destroyed? Go behind it and up those stairs. What's there? Go and see for yourself if you want to find out.' His gags did not work all that often, because he was known for being a piss-taker, but still they gave him the aura of someone who knew his stuff.

The excitement of the hunt had seized hold of everyone. When I met Orazi, all cheerful and excited, making me feel his pockets, I realized that there was nobody that would have understood us, me and Biancone. But there were two of us, we understood each other, and this fact would always keep us together.

'Feel here, feel here! Know what that is?'

'Bottles?'

'Valves! Philips valves. I'll make a new radio with them.'

'Good luck!'

'Happy hunting!'

Moving from house to house, we went into older, poorer areas. The stairs were narrow; from the state of the mess in them, the rooms looked as if they had been ransacked years and years before and left to decay in the wind blowing from the sea. The dishes in a sink were dirty; the saucepans were greasy and congealed, and perhaps had been spared because of that.

I had gone into that house with a group of other Avanguardisti. And I noticed that Biancone was not amongst them. I asked: 'Have you seen where Biancone went?'

'Eh?' they replied, 'Why? He certainly wasn't with our group.'

We had got involved with several gangs, which every so often would split up and mingle with others; and I couldn't say at what point, while thinking I was following the gang with Biancone in it, I had taken a wrong turning. 'Biancone!' I called up the stairs. 'Biancone!' I shouted down a stretch of corridor. I thought I heard voices, I don't know where from. I opened a door. I was in an artisan's shed. There was a carpenter's bench down one side and, in the middle of the room, a table used by someone who did inlay work or worked with ebony. There were still shavings on the ground, splinters of wood, cigarette-butts, as if he had stopped work two minutes previously; and above it, scattered around and in pieces, were the hundreds of tools and bits of work that the man had made: frames, cases, backs of chairs, and God knows how many umbrella handles.

Evening was starting to fall. In the middle of the room hung a light-shade with a pear-shaped counterweight, but no bulb. And in the light from the sunset coming from the little window I looked at a shelf on which were lined up, all in a row, some busts of dolls to be used as Aunt Sallies, I think, or for a little mechanical puppet theatre: the wooden heads had been carved in a style that hinted at a naïve taste for caricature – some were painted, but most of them were still in their raw state. Just a few of these heads had met the same fate as everything else in the room and had been knocked off their necks; the majority of them were still there, with their lips curved in an inexpressive smile and their round eyes wide open, and one of them actually seemed to me to move, swaying on the upright peg that was its neck, perhaps shaken by the breeze from the tiny window, or by my sudden entrance.

Or had someone been in there shortly before and touched it? I opened yet another door. There was a bed, an untouched cradle; a cupboard wide open and empty. I went into another room: on the floor there was a sea of letters, postcards, photographs. I saw a photograph of an engaged couple: he was a soldier, she was a small blonde. I crouched down to read a letter: '*Ma chérie . . .*' It was her room. There was little light, but with one knee on the ground I started to decipher the letter, and after the first page I began to look for the second. A group of Young Fascist sailors burst in, out of breath and all peering forward like bloodhounds; they crowded around me: 'What is it, what have you found?' 'Nothing, nothing,' I muttered. They sifted the heap of papers with their hands and feet, and then rushed out with the same breathlessness with which they had come in.

I could not see to read any more. From the window the noise of the sea could be heard as if it were in the houses themselves. I went out into the open. It was getting dark. I headed towards the assembly point. In the streets there were other comrades heading that way, with their jerkins deformed by humps and with the less easy to hide objects wrapped up in improvised bundles. 'And what about you, what did you take?' they asked me.

Assembly was in a pavilion that had previously been an English club, but was now transformed into the Fascist Club. In its corridors illuminated by chandeliers it was like a fair: everyone was showing and boasting about his booty, without fear of their superiors any more, and was plotting the best way of hiding it so as not to be too noticeable on returning to Italy. Bergamini made the tennis racquet disappear into the baggy part of his trousers, and Ceretti was cloaking his chest with bicycle inner-tubes, over which he put a jumper, and looked like Mr Universe. In the midst of them all I saw Biancone. He had some women's stockings in his hands and was taking them out from their cellophane wrapper to show them, making them snake through the air like serpents.

'How many have you got?' they asked.

'Six pairs!'

'Silk?'

'You bet!'

'Good haul! Who're you going to give them to? A present?'

'A present? I can go womanising free for a month now!'

There: Biancone too; now I was on my own.

The others were cursing because they had been there God knows how many times and only Biancone had been clever enough to unearth those stockings.

'The stockings?' he said, 'but what about my tartan scarf, now? And my cherry-wood pipe?' He was top-class, Biancone, he was always the one with the sure touch, the one who always discovered a treasure wherever he laid his hands.

I went over to congratulate him, and maybe I was being sincere. Basically, I had been a fool not to take anything; they were not anyone else's possessions any more. He winked at me and showed me his real finds, the ones he really cared about and would not show the others: a pendant with a picture of Danielle Darrieux, a book by Léon Blum, and also a moustache-curler. That was it: you just had to do things with style like Biancone: I had not been able to. The Commander himself was also having fun reviewing the booty taken by the Avanguardisti; he felt their jerkins, got them to bring out a whole range of items. Bizantini followed him, and laughingly agreed with him, very satisfied with us. Then he summoned us all, made us assemble around him, without making us form ranks, in order to give us our instructions. There was an atmosphere of glee, excitement, and everyone had that funfair of goods on them.

'The arrival of our Spanish comrades', Bizantini said, 'is estimated at nine-thirty this evening. Assembly will be here at 8.45 p.m. to put ourselves in good order and be armed. After that we shall be off, and by tonight we will be back home. We will find a way of hiding this stuff, you'll see, either in the bus or on you, and nobody's going to object. The

Commander, who is extremely proud of you, has assured me of this. Boys, let's not forget, this is a conquered city and we are the conquerors. Everything in it belongs to us, and no one can object to that! Now we still have an hour and a quarter: you can go off again, but no noise, no carry-on, just as you have done up to now, off and hunt for what you want. I tell you this,' he added, in a louder voice, 'that any young man who is here today and does not take away something is a fool! Yes, sir, a fool, and I would be ashamed to shake his hand!'

A murmur of applause greeted these last sentences. And I was trembling with excitement: I was the only one, the only one amongst all of them, not to have taken anything, the only one who would not take anything, who would go back home empty-handed! It was not that I was less ready or sharp than the others, as I had doubted up until a few moments previously: mine was a courageous, almost heroic attitude! It was I who was full of myself now, more than they were.

Bizantini was still talking, giving his pointless advice to the impatient Avanguardisti. I was close to a door; in its lock was the key: a hotel key with a huge pendant showing its room number and the words 'New Club'. I slipped the key from its lock. There: I would take away that key as a souvenir, a Fascist key. I slid it into my pocket. That would be my booty.

These were our last hours in Menton. I walked on my own, towards the sea. It was dark. From the houses the cries of my comrades reached me. I was seized by a gloomy turn of thought. I went towards a bench; and I saw that seated on it was someone in a sailor's uniform. I recognized the yellow and crimson tassel of the Young Fascists under his collar: he was one of the young sailors from ***. I sat down; he stayed with his chin on his chest.

'Hey,' I said, and I still didn't know what I was going to say to him, 'are you not going off round the houses too?'

He did not even turn round. 'I don't give a toss,' he said quietly.

'Didn't you take anything?' I asked.

He repeated: 'I don't give a toss.'

'Tell me, are you not taking anything because you didn't find anything or because you don't want to?'

'I don't give a toss,' he said again; he got up, went off with long strides and his arms hanging down, amid the pointed shadows of the pine trees. All of a sudden he started to sing, but more shouting than singing, at the top of his voice: '*Vivereee! Finché c'è gioventù . . .*' Was he drunk?

I sat down on the bench, took the key out of my pocket and stared at it in contemplation. I would have liked to have given some symbolic meaning to it. 'New Club', then Fascist Club, and now in my possession: what could that mean? I wanted it to be a really important, indispensable key, so that when they didn't find it they would go mad, they would be unable to lock a room that contained some vast secret treasure, or documents on which their own personal fates depended.

I got up and headed back towards the Fascist Club.

There were a few Avanguardisti in the corridors packing up their knick-knacks; the corporals were counting the rifles and deciding on the layout of the squadrons; Biancone was there too, with them. I went along the corridors pretending I was bored, running my hand along the wall and the doors, whistling something that was like a dance tune. Every time my hand came across a key, I slid it swiftly from the lock and hid it in my hunting jacket. The corridors were full of doors, and nearly every one had its key hanging out of it, with the gold number dangling downwards. By now my jacket was full of them. I could see no other keys around. No one had noticed me. I went out.

At the door I met some others who were coming in. 'Well, what are you taking home?' 'Me? . . . Nothing . . .' But they saw the smile about my lips. 'Oh, yeah, well done, nothing . . .' they said.

I roamed around the garden. I must have had twenty keys on me. They clanked like old iron. 'I've got my hoard too, now,' I thought. 'Hey, you, what have you got on you?' someone passing by asked me. 'You sound like an Alpine cow!'

I slunk away. The garden had pergolas and bowers covered with neglected climbing plants, and I went in amongst them. I started to realize what I had done. My incomprehensible act could, for one reason or another, be discovered at any time. What if some officer or local leader of ours needed to lock something in one of those half-empty rooms? . . . And what if my comrades – now or later, in the coach, or in Italy – forced me to show what I had in my jacket? . . . All those keys, with the room numbers of the 'New Club' on them, could only have been stolen from the Fascist Club: and to what end? How could I have justified my actions? It was clearly a gesture of disrespect, or rebellion, or sabotage . . . The former 'New Club' loomed up behind me with all its windows lit up, but with blackout blinds from which only vague blue glimmers could be seen. I was a saboteur of Fascism in conquered territory . . .

I ran on. I had seen a stretch of water twinkling: in the middle of a flower bed there was a pond surrounded by rocks, with, in the middle, a dried-up fountain. One by one I took the keys out of my jacket and dropped them into the water, immersing them gently so no clank could be heard. From the bottom of the pond a murky cloud arose, cancelling out the reflections of the moon. After the last key was at the bottom, I saw a pale shadow pass by in the water: a fish, maybe an old goldfish, was coming to see what on earth had happened.

I got up. Had I been a coward? Putting my hands into my pockets, I noticed I still had one more key: the first one I had taken and which must have stayed in my pocket. I felt myself in danger once more, and happy. My comrades were coming back for assembly, and I was with them.

An hour after we had been lined up in the station square the train containing the Spanish Falangists arrived. Bizantini roared: 'Present arms!' There were weak lamps that had been blacked out underneath the station roof. The Young Falangists formed ranks in that area of light, and we were very far off, down at the far end of the piazza. They were tall and strong, with what seemed to us squashed faces, like those of boxers; their red berets were drawn down over one eye, their black jerseys rolled up at the elbow, and their small rucksacks were fastened to their belts. A wind was blowing with short, sudden gusts, the lights swayed, we held up our rifles with bayonets attached facing the Caudillo's young soldiers. At times we could hear the notes and cadences of one of their marches, which they had not stopped singing from the time they arrived, something like '*Arò* . . . *arò* . . . *arò* . . .' They received some typically clipped orders from their superiors in their own language, and they formed ranks, measuring their distance from each other by stretching their arms forwards; and we could hear them calling and shouting at each other, though not very clearly: 'Sebastian . . . Habla, Vincente . . .' Then they marched off, reached the coaches that were waiting for them, and got on. They left just as they had arrived: without ever glancing at us.

When the time came for us to leave, we were all laden like smugglers as we passed in front of Bizantini, who examined us one by one to make sure we did not stick out too much. He sent each one off with a slap on their jackets, which jingled with the objects inside, or with a kick on the backside. I went past him as well, my empty jacket making my uniform seem close-fitting and smooth, and I kept my eyes up, looking straight at Bizantini, while he stood in a serious pose, saying nothing before moving on to joke with the person coming after.

The coach went back along the coast; we were all tired and silent. The darkness was cut through every so often by the headlights of motor columns; the houses on our coastline were dark, the sea empty, silvery and threatening. The war was on, and all of us were caught up in it, and by now I knew that it would be the decisive factor in our lives, in my life; though I did not know exactly how.

UNPA Nights

As a boy, I was a bit of a slow developer; when I was sixteen, given my age, I was rather behind in many things. Then, all of a sudden, in the summer of 1940, I wrote a three-act play, had a love affair and learnt to ride a bicycle. But I still had not spent a night away from home when the order came round that, during the holidays, high-school pupils were to go on night duty once a week with the UNPA.*

The school buildings in the town had to be protected whenever there was an air raid. However, there had not been any air-raids up until then, and this UNPA business seemed just another formality, like so many others. For me it was something new and exciting; it was September, nearly all my schoolfriends were still away, either on holiday or hunting in the hills, or they had been evacuated in June and had not yet come back. Only Biancone and I were left in town: I would wander around during the day bored out of my mind, and he would wander around all night, having a tremendous time – or so it seemed. These shifts with the

* During the war, the UNPA (Unione Nazionale per la Protezione Anti-aerea) was the Italian Anti-aircraft Corps.

UNPA had to be done in pairs. Biancone and I, of course, made sure we enrolled together: he would take me to all the places he knew; we were going to have a great time. We were assigned the primary school building and a shift on the Friday night. A room with two camp beds and a telephone was our guard room there at the school; our task was always to be ready, in case of air-raid alarms; we could also make inspections nearby: in other words, go out as much as we wanted, but just one of us at a time, because they were going to phone to check up. Naturally, we instantly thought that we could also go out together if we squared it with those in charge, and that we could use the telephone in the early hours of the morning primarily to play tricks on people we knew.

But, however much we said 'We'll do this and that! You'll see what fun we'll have!', and however much we felt we had planned and anticipated everything imaginable in the days leading up to that Friday, nevertheless I expected something more from that night, something I could still not articulate: a new revelation, though as yet I did not know what it would be, the revelation of the night. For Biancone, on the other hand, everything seemed cheerily routine and predictable, and I also pretended that it was the same for me, but, in the meantime, in my imagination, I could feel the unknown time of night foaming like an invisible sea around each of our vague projects.

That Friday I went out after dinner, and it was still just an evening like any other. I was carrying my pyjamas with me and a pillowcase to put over the pillow of the camp bed where

I would sleep. I also had a magazine with pictures, because, amongst the many activities planned, we would also spend some of the time reading.

The school was a big stone building, with a corrugated iron roof. It rose high above the road, in a rather unfortunate position, and you reached it by three sets of steps. It had been built by the regime, but it did not reflect at all the stiff architecture of that time: it breathed an air of bureaucratic predictability which the lukewarm Fascism of my town tried to maintain as far as possible. Even the bas-relief on the façade, which actually showed a Fascist Scout and Girl Guide sitting on either side of the words 'Town School', seemed to be inspired more by a pedagogical sobriety that smacked entirely of the nineteenth century.

It was a moonless night. The school building still reflected a vague brightness. I had arranged to meet Biancone there, but of course he was not on time. Beyond the school, in the darkness, there were houses and fields. You could hear the sound of crickets and frogs. I could no longer muster my enthusiasm for the whole thing, the enthusiasm that had brought me thus far. Now, wandering back and forth beneath that primary school, on my own, with my pyjamas, a pillow case and an illustrated magazine in my hand, I felt out of place and embarrassed.

I was standing there waiting when suddenly a flame shot up, licking my back. I jumped: the magazine I was holding under my arm had caught fire; I dropped it, and even before I could get frightened, I realized it was one of Biancone's tricks. Flat against the wall, he was still holding in his hand the match with which he had crept up on me in the dark. He was not laughing. As always, he had an impeccably official look about him as he said:

'Excuse me, you UNPA people, you haven't by any chance seen a fire around here?'

'Yes, a fire that I hope burns your bum!' I began swearing, and with my heel I stamped out the blazing magazine. 'What kind of trick is that?'

'It was not a trick. It's an inspection. My dear chap, the UNPA means a life full of danger: one must be ready for anything. However, I've seen that you keep guard well. Well done. Bye. I can now go off, then, and see to my own business.'

I told him not to play the wise guy, that we had to go up and see our guardroom and dump our stuff.

But the school doors were closed. If you flattened the bell with your hand, you could only hear a distant drrring sound; if you knocked, you heard nothing but the echoes of empty corridors.

'There's nobody there! The caretaker woman lives out in the country!' said a voice behind us, perhaps alarmed at our hammering on the door. We turned round and, up there on a wall, amid the shadows of bean plants, was the outline of a man; he was pouring from a watering can a liquid that we recognised from its smell as liquid manure. He was a vegetable gardener, taking advantage of the nocturnal hours to fertilize his plants without disturbing his neighbours with the stench.

'But we demand entry! We are the UNPA!'

'Who?'

'The UNPA!'

In a little cottage, a tiny light suddenly went out. Biancone nudged me, satisfied with this proof of our authority. 'See what it means?' he said quietly, 'We're the UNPA.'

'The caretaker's in the country because she's afraid of the alarms,' said the plant-waterer in the dark above us, 'but she's not far away: if you go up that road, at the top you'll see a one-storey house. Call out "Bigìn!" and she'll answer.'

'Thank you.'

'Not at all. By the way . . . seeing you are from the UNPA, can we keep that blue light there, or is it forbidden?'

'That's fine, fine,' we replied grudgingly, 'it's a bit too bright, but you can keep it . . .'

Biancone said quietly to me: 'That stink: will we tell him?'

'What?'

'That it's forbidden. It'll attract enemy war planes.'

'Don't be silly, come on,' and we went up the cobbled street that climbed into the countryside.

From the few houses there emerged thin shafts of blue light and muffled sounds: voices raised, the clatter of dishes, children crying. The night outside was the reverse of the night at home: we were now the unknown footsteps echoing in the street, the whistled tune that those who haven't fallen asleep try to follow as it moves away and dies out.

There was a light at the caretaker's house. In order to establish a tone of authority, Biancone shouted out: 'Lights! Lights!', but here the light stayed on.

'Bigìn!' we shouted again, 'Bigìn!'

'Who is it?'

'The key! We want the key to the school!'

'Who are you?'

'We're the UNPA! Lights! Hey, that light!'

A shutter opened, the light flooded the full square of the window without anything to screen it, and opened up the coloured vista of a kitchen with its copperware and enamel jugs and cups hanging on the walls, and Bigìn said: 'Oh, stop pestering me!' In her hand she held a knife dripping red drops, and half a tomato. She slammed the shutter, the darkness returned and we stood there blinded.

Bigìn came towards us beneath a low pergola. There was a rack made of reeds on which she slowly placed the tomatoes in order to cover them with salt. She was a small, dark woman, whose high chignon hairstyle gave her an imposing air. She stayed there beneath the pergola and continued salting the tomatoes in the darkness, with confident actions, as if she could actually see.

She was suspicious of us; either that or she didn't want to move. 'Are you really the people from the UNPA?'

'Of course, look: we've even got our pyjamas,' said Biancone, as if this was a completely logical response, and he unrolled from his package a pair of pyjama trousers with coloured stripes, holding them out in front of himself as if trying to prove that they were exactly his size.

The caretaker did not seem to find anything to object to in that bizarre proof of identity. She merely said: 'But why isn't the teacher there, Belluomo?'

Belluomo was a young man, the primary schoolteacher,

who presided over this very business of guard duty.

'Because we're here instead. It was he who sent us.'

Finally the caretaker left her tomatoes and dried her hands on her apron. We said to her not to worry, all we needed were the keys; but no chance, she insisted on coming to show us everything herself, because we didn't know the place. 'Have you got a torch?'

'No, we can see in the dark, we UNPA people.'

'It doesn't matter, I've got one,' and from the pockets of her huge apron she took out a small, battery-operated torch, made of tin, and shone a cone of light, which started to move in front of her feet like the tip of a stick, before she took a step.

So we went down that cobbled hill, between little walls sheltering kitchen gardens and vines, the two of us following our slow-moving caretaker.

'You didn't tell me,' I said to Biancone, 'that you were taking me to spend the night in the country.'

Without saying anything Biancone disappeared.

The caretaker spun the torch round. 'Where's he gone, the other chap?'

'How should I know?'

Biancone suddenly jumped down from a little wall, almost landing on the caretaker. He had two bunches of grapes in his hand. 'Here, eat this,' he said, throwing one of them to me.

'A fine way to behave!' said the caretaker. 'If the owner sees you, he'll take a pot shot at you!'

Now, suddenly, we were the night-time fruit thieves, the ones my father always threatened to shoot with his salt-rifle, while my childish legal-minded imagination tried in vain to give them a face. Suddenly the lawlessness of the night took on once more that distant image from my childhood years.

'Fine way to behave!' the caretaker repeated.

'Hey, a chicken coop!' said Biancone, turning to me. 'Eh, what do you say?'

In the moonless sky the soft shadows of bats could just about be made out. Dark moths fluttered around the care-taker's torch. A toad crossing the road stopped, dazzled by the light. 'Hey, be careful or you'll crush it!' No chance; it slipped away between her feet.

We came to a point where the countryside ended and you could sense the expanse of town roofs down below. 'Now she'll jump on her broom and fly over the city,' I thought. But the caretaker was already leading us to the school door and opening up.

Without switching on the light, she took us along the corridors and stairs. We passed a succession of classroom doorways and wall charts. The caretaker looked around apprehensively, as though fearful of leaving us in charge of those rooms and objects which cost her so much labour to clean and put in order.

She made us climb many stairs and opened our lodgings up for us, then disappeared. As we took possession of the room, we heard her clacking along the corridors grumbling, first on one floor, then on another. 'What's she doing? Locking everything up? Or does she want to stay the night too and keep guard?'

All of a sudden, down on the ground floor, the main door creaked on its hinges and the lock slammed shut.

'Has she gone?'

'And she's not left us the key? She's closed us in! The witch!'

We went to look at the windows of the ground floor, but those without iron gratings were too high off the ground, not so much that you couldn't jump down, but high enough not to allow you to climb back up.

We got onto the phone to see if we could find that Belluomo guy, who must have had a key as well. We woke his mother at his house, but he wasn't there; in the other schools, where there must have been people mobilized like ourselves, there was no response; at the Young Fascists' Hall and at the Fascist Club, nothing. We disturbed or woke up half the town and we then ended up finding him in a café, where we were phoning to ask if we could bet on the billiards matches over the phone.

'Oh, yes, I'll come right away,' said the poor wretch.

While we were waiting for him, we did a tour of the school, going into the classrooms and the gym, but we found nothing interesting, and could not switch on the lights, since the blackout blinds for the windows were nearly all missing. We went to stretch out on our camp beds, to read and smoke.

The magazine that Biancone had half burned was full of photographs of English cities, seen from the air, with bombs falling on them in clusters. We did not know what it meant and we leafed through the pages absent-mindedly. Then there was an account of the whole story of King Carol of Rumania, because there had been a coup d'état at that time and they had changed king. The article was amusing, especially for us, who were not used to reading about court or political intrigues in the newspapers. I read it out loud to Biancone. There was the story of La Lupescu, which we commented on with laughter and shouts of excitement, not so much for the story in itself as for that name: Lupescu, which sounded so softly feral and full of dark shadows.*

'La Lupescu! La Lupescu!' we shouted, standing up on our camp beds.

'La Lupescu!' I shouted, along the echoing corridors and leaning out of the windows, watching the dark mantle of night, which I had not yet succeeded in wrapping round myself.

Biancone had found two gas masks. 'These are for us!' We instantly struggled to put them over our faces. Breathing was difficult, and the inside of the masks had an unpleasant smell of rubber and of storage, but they were objects not totally unfamiliar to us, because, right from when we were children at school, it had been drummed into us as an article of faith how useful gas masks were in defending oneself from any (or rather from probable) attacks from asphyxiating gas. So, with our heads transformed into those of enormous ants seen through a microscope, we communicated in inarticulate grunts as we wandered around half-blind through the hallways of the school. We also found some helmets, of the old kind, from the First World War, some hatchets, and torches with blue blackout filters. By now our UNPA outfits were complete; we armed ourselves to the teeth and filed along the corridors on parade, singing a marching tune: 'Un-pà!

* *Lupa* is Italian for she-wolf.

Un-pà!', which, however, sounded through the gas masks as a confused 'Uhà! Uhà!'

'U-e-u!' mooed Biancone, wrapping himself in a huge window curtain and making sinuous movements.

'Uh! Uh!' I answered him, raising the hatchet as if in a war cry.

Biancone made a sign saying no. 'U-e-u!' he enunciated slowly again, emphasizing his lascivious hip-swaying.

'Ah!' I enthusiastically understood. 'Lupescu! La Lupescu!' and we started to act out some scenes from a gas-masked version of the life of King Carol and his lover.

The bell rang. It was Belluomo. We signalled to each other to keep quiet. Without making a noise, we went down to the classrooms on the ground floor. Belluomo was still ringing the bell and knocking. We had left open the ground-floor windows, from where we had previously studied our escape route. We popped our heads out of two different windows, with our gas masks, our helmets, and anti-mustard-gas gloves on, Biancone with a hatchet in his hand, I with the hose from a pump. Belluomo was a young man, low in build, blond, skinny in his uniform, that of a First Lieutenant in the Young Fascists, with his safari jacket and boots. Fed up with ringing the bell and not seeing any sign of life nor any lights on, he made as if to leave. Biancone struck the window sill three times with his hatchet. Belluomo turned round towards the window and saw the outline of someone looking out. 'Hey!' he said, 'Is that you, Biancone?' We stayed silent. He lit his torch and pointed it towards the window sill. 'Oh!' He had lit up the gas mask and hatchet. 'Hey, what have you got there? Are you crazy?' Just at that moment he heard a splash of water. From a high window a jet of water was cascading down, spreading out onto the pavement. I had connected the pump to a tap.

People were passing by on the street and they stopped when they saw all that commotion. Belluomo had immediately turned his light towards my window. He was in time to see my gas mask appear, my gloved hands withdrawing the hose and disappearing.

He re-directed the strip of light towards the first window, but there was no one there any more. The passers-by had gathered round him. 'What is it? Gas? Gas attacks?' He did not want to say it was probably a trick, as that would look as if he was losing face; and, in any case, he was not even quite sure what was going on; he was a fussy type of guy, with no sense of humour.

'There! Up there!' said a passer-by, and pointed towards a third-floor window. He had seen one of those silent gas mask ghosts. Belluomo tried to reach it with the light of his electric torch. It disappeared. 'Hey! You idiots! Come down!' Another ghost appeared on the fourth floor. 'What's going on?' asked the passers-by. 'Is there a gas attack in the school?' And Belluomo replied, 'No, it's nothing . . .' We continued appearing and disappearing from those windows. 'Is it manoeuvres?' people were asking. 'It's nothing, nothing, move along, move along,' and he sent them away. We had had enough fun and stopped.

This Belluomo guy had no authority at all. He was a good sort, it has to be said, or at least he did not have enough memory or enthusiasm to be vindictive with us. 'Hey, what have you been up to? Are you mad? This is really a bit of craziness,' he started to reproach us, with his plaintive tone and weary insults, but already you could tell that the little amount of feeling there was in him was quickly evaporating, because in his head everything tended to be played down and made little of. Our spectacular mockery of his authority and of our duties was completely wasted on him: he treated us with that familiar tone of annoyance that is typical of the primary teacher who cannot keep discipline. So, after a few nagging reproaches, he proceeded to hand over the equipment, which, in any case, we had already tried out on our own, and to explain our duties to us. He led us up to the attics and showed us the boxes of sand for spreading, in case we had to neutralize incendiary bombs.

He was much more assured of himself and seemed to have gone back to being aware of his authority. He handed over the key, warning us not to leave the building unguarded for any reason.

'Yes, sir, yes, sir, we'll do as you say . . . We're now going out together in search of women,' Biancone said to him, in his unflappable manner.

Belluomo opened his mouth, frowned, shrugged his shoulders and wandered off grumbling. He had gone back to being gloomy and unhappy.

Shortly afterwards we went out. It was after midnight. That warm darkness without stars or wind continued. Almost nobody was around in the streets. In the main square, beneath the blinking traffic light, there was the outline of a smallish man, the little point of his cigarette glowing. Biancone recognized him from his stance, with his hands in his pockets and his legs akimbo. He was a friend of his, Palladiani, a great night-bird. Biancone whistled the tune of a song which must have held some special meaning for them; the other man continued humming the rest of it, as though in a sudden burst of euphoria. We went up to him. Biancone wanted to scrounge a cigarette off him, but Palladiani said he didn't have any and actually managed to scrounge one off Biancone. In the light of his match I noticed the pale face of a young man who had aged before his time.

He said he was waiting for a certain Ketty, who was well known to Biancone: she had gone to a party in a big house, and now must have been on her way back. 'Unless she decides to stay there,' he said, suddenly laughing and humming a foxtrot tune. He also mentioned how, seeing some girl called Lori with another called Rosetta, he had made a suggestive remark to her which I didn't understand but which Biancone clearly appreciated a lot. Then he asked us, 'And have you heard the new tricks to play in the blackout?' 'No,' we said, and he explained them to us. We were very enthusiastic about them, and instantly wanted to put them into practice. But Palladiani, because of some mysterious commitments, said goodbye and went off singing to himself.

The blackout tricks included, for example, this: the two of us would walk quickly along with our cigarettes lit; we would see a single person coming towards us along the same pavement from the opposite direction; then, while continuing to walk alongside each other, one of us would raise our right hand, the other the left, holding our lit cigarettes out at head height; the passer-by would see the two glowing cigarette tips at some distance from each other and would think he could pass between them, but, in fact, he would suddenly find his path blocked by two people and would be trapped there like an idiot. Then you could also do the opposite: walk along apart from each other at the two edges of the pavement, and instead hold our cigarettes close to each other, between us; the passer-by, thinking that we were walking right along the centre of the pavement, would move to the side, thus crashing into one of us; he would mutter 'Oh, I'm sorry', and move to the other side, where he would crash into the other person.

We spent a pleasant hour or so in these games, as long as we found the right passers-by. Some of them, disorientated, would say sorry, others uttered swear words or threatened to start a fight, but we quickly nipped out of the way. I would be worried each time, imagining each passer-by coming towards us to be a weird night-bird, people with knives, dodgy drunks. Instead they turned out to be respectable people suffering from insomnia, who were taking their hunting dog for a walk, or pallid gamblers coming back from the card game, or workers from the night shift at the gasworks. We nearly played the trick on two carabinieri, who gave us a dirty look. 'Everything under control round here?' Biancone asked them brazenly, as I tried to pull him away by his shirt sleeve.

'What? What do you want?'

'We're from the UNPA, on duty,' Biancone replied; 'I was just saying was everything under control?'

'Eh, yes, yes, all under control.' They said goodbye, not entirely convinced, and went off.

And we also would have liked to find women on their own, but there weren't any, apart from an ageing prostitute with whom the ruse didn't work, because she tended not to avoid but to enjoy walking into people. We lit a match to examine her and immediately put it out. After a very short chat we let her go.

More than in the main streets these tricks were good to play in the smaller ones, which were narrow and dark, with steps in them, the ones that came down from the old town. But there the fun was already in the shadows, the pattern of arches and railings in the area, the close huddle of houses we didn't know, the night itself, and we stopped mucking about with our cigarettes.

Already from the discussion with Palladiani I had realized that Biancone was not in fact that connoisseur of nightlife that I had taken him for. He was always in a bit too much of a hurry to say 'Yes . . . I know . . . No, you don't say, not her!' at every name Palladiani mentioned, anxious to show he was in the know; and certainly he was, on the whole, but his knowledge was clearly a superficial and patchy smattering compared with the perfect mastery displayed by Palladiani. In fact, I had watched with some regret as Palladiani went off, thinking that he and he alone, not Biancone, could introduce me into the heart of that world. Now I would watch every move by Biancone with a critical eye, waiting to regain my original confidence in him, or to lose it for ever.

Certainly, I felt a sense of disillusionment with this nocturnal walk of ours. Or at least, an impression that was the opposite of what I expected. We were wandering along a poor, narrow street; there was no one around; all the lights were out in the houses; and yet we felt we were in the midst of so many people. The windows scattered randomly over the dark walls were either open or just half-shut, and from each of them emerged low breathing or sometimes a deep snoring, and also the tick of alarm clocks, and the dripping of taps in sinks. We were in the street, but the noises were the noises of the house, of a hundred houses all together; and even the windless air had that heaviness that human sleep causes to sit solidly in bedrooms.

The presence of unknown people sleeping arouses a natural respect in honest minds, and in spite of ourselves we were intimidated by this. And that cracked, irregular concerto of breathing, and the ticking of the clocks, and the poverty of the houses, gave the impression of precarious, troubled rest; and the signs of the war that you could see all around – blue lights, poles propping up walls, piles of sandbags, arrows pointing the way to shelters, and even our very own presence – all this seemed a threat to the sleep of exhausted people. So we had lowered our voices, and without noticing it had abandoned our role as noisy jokers, rebels against the rules, violators of all human decency. The feeling that now dominated us was a kind of complicity with unknown people, who were asleep behind those walls, the feeling of having discovered some secret of theirs, and of knowing how to respect it.

The street finished at a stairway with an iron banister, and, at the bottom, in the uncertain light shed by the moon, there was an empty square, with the market stalls and trestles all piled up. And all around it lay the amphitheatre of old houses swollen with sleep and breathing.

From a street that went down to the square came the sounds of footsteps and singing. It was a raucous chorus, made up of voices that had no harmony or warmth, accompanied by a stamping of boots. Down came a group of the Fascist militia, middle-aged people, one behind the other, and others in a group running up and joining them: the latter were in black shirts underneath the coarse grey-green military uniform, carrying shotguns and rucksacks. They were singing a vulgar refrain, but with some hesitation and shyness, as though they were forcing themselves, now that night time had released them from any semblance of discipline, to show off their true nature as soldiers of fortune, enemies of everyone and totally above the law.

Their irruption into that space brought in a gust of violence; my skin crawled as though suddenly I had been plunged into civil war, a war whose fire had always stayed lit beneath the ashes and, from time to time, would spit out tongues of fire.

'Look at that lot!' said Biancone, and standing still against the banister we watched them march off in the empty square, which echoed to their footsteps.

'Where have they come from, yes, where have they come from? What's up there?' I asked, convinced that they had emerged from some brothel or other, whereas maybe they were a squadron returning from a pointless tour of guard duty in the mountains, from some manoeuvres exercise.

'Up there? Ah, yes, there must be . . .' replied Biancone, betraying once more his limited competence. 'Come with me, I know where to take you!'

The appearance of the soldiers had broken that atmosphere of tranquillity that had stood over us: now we were tense, excited, with a need for action, for something unpredictable.

We went down the steps towards the piazza.

'Where are we going?' I asked.

'Ah! To La Lupescu!' he replied.

'La Lupescu!' I shouted, and I stood aside, because there was a man climbing up the steps, stooped, with his grey hair almost totally shaved off, in shirt sleeves, going up and supporting himself with a big, knotted hand clutching the banister. The man, without looking us in the face, but continuing his climb, said in a loud baritone voice: 'Workers . . .'

Biancone was already mumbling a reply – something along the lines that there was no reason to take the piss, that we were workers too, in our own way – when the old man, who meanwhile had got to the top of the steps, added, still in a loud voice, but in a bass timbre '. . . unite!'

Biancone and I stopped.

'Did you hear that?'

'Yes . . .'

'He must be a communist?'

'"Workers, unite!" He's a communist, did you hear?'

'But did he not look more like a drunk?'

'Not a bit of it: he was walking straight up. He's a communist! The old town is full of them!'

'Let's go and talk to him!'

'Good idea! Let's catch him up!'

We turned round and flew up the steps.

'But what will we say to him?'

'First, we'll make him realize that with us he can talk . . .
Then we'll ask him to explain that phrase to us . . .'

But the man wasn't there any more: from that point several
narrow streets went off; we ran from one to the other,
randomly; he had disappeared; we couldn't work out where
he had gone in such a short time; but we never found him
again.

We were full of curiosity and excitement: excited to aban-
don the reins, to do new, forbidden things. But the image in
which this imprecise desire expressed itself most easily was
that of sex, and so we headed off to the house of someone
called Meri-meri.

This Meri-meri lived in a low house, on the edge between
the clutter of housing in the old town and the kitchen gardens
of the countryside, and on the ground floor it had stable
quarters for carters. The cobbled street came out from under
a dark archway, and after Meri-meri's house it continued,
flanked by a metal fence beyond which a mass of rubbish
spilled down an uncultivated slope.

I went with Biancone to just beneath her house: at one of
its windows light filtered from behind a thick curtain. Biancone whistled twice, then called out: 'Meri-meri!'

The curtain rose up and at the window there appeared the

white of a woman: a long face, it seemed, surrounded by the black of her hair, and her shoulders and arms: 'What is it? Who are you?'

'La Lupescu!' I whispered to Biancone. 'Tell me, is that La Lupescu there?'

Biancone tried to put himself under the light cast by a pale street lamp. 'It's me, do you recognize me? Yes, of course you do, I came the other week! I'm here with a friend. Will you let us come up?'

'No. I can't.' She lowered the curtain again.

Biancone whistled again, and called out. 'Meri-meri! Oh, Meri-meri!' He started to hammer on the door with his fists. 'She must open up, for God's sake! Why doesn't she?'

The woman appeared again. This time she had a cigarette in her mouth. 'I've got company. Come back in an hour.' We stayed for a while listening, until we heard that there really must have been a man in her room.

We started to wander off again. Now we were in a street between the old areas and the newer ones, where the old, tall houses had dubious modern-city paintwork.

'This is a good street,' said Biancone. A shadow came towards us: it was a little bald man, in sandals, dressed in a pair of trousers and a vest, despite the cool hour of the morning, and with a thin, dark scarf tied around his neck.

'Hey, youngsters,' he said in a whisper, his two round eyes, surrounded by thick black eyebrows, staring at us ,'do you want to have sex? Do you want to go to Pierina? Eh? If you want, I can give you her address . . .'

'No, no,' we said, 'we're already fixed up.'

'Pierina's lovely, you know? Eh?' The little man wheezed into our faces with those demonic eyes.

But we had spotted someone else coming along the centre of the street, a lame girl, not beautiful, with one of those then fashionable crew-neck sweaters and her hair cut short. She had stopped some distance from us. We dodged past the little bald man and went up to the girl. She held out her hand with a sheet of paper in it. 'Who is Signor Biancone?' she asked, in a whisper. Biancone took the piece of paper. In the light of a street lamp we read the following words, written in a neat hand, like that of a schoolboy: 'Do you know the pleasure of love? Vito Palladiani.'

The meaning of the message and the way it had been delivered to us were mysterious, but Palladiani's style was unmistakable.

'Where is Palladiani?' we asked the girl.

She smiled awkwardly. 'Come with me.'

She went into a dark doorway and we went up a steep stairway that had no landings. She knocked at a door with a coded knock. The door opened. There was a room with flowery upholstery, an old woman all made up, sitting in an armchair, and a gramophone with a trumpet horn in a corner. The limping girl opened a door and we went into another room, full of people and smoke. They were standing around a table where others were playing cards. Nobody turned to look at us. The room was entirely closed and the smoke so thick you could hardly see, while the heat was such that everyone was sweating. In the circle of people standing watching the others play cards there were also some women, not pretty or young; one was in her bra and underskirt. Meanwhile, the limping girl had led us into a kind of Japanese sitting room.

'But where is Palladiani?' we asked.

'He's coming now,' she said, and left us there.

We were examining this place when Palladiani arrived in a great hurry, carrying in his arms a heap of crumpled sheets. 'My dearest friends, how are things?' he said, all cheerful, as always. He was in his shirt sleeves and wearing a garish bow tie that I was certain he was not wearing when we had met him in the street.

'Have you seen Dolores? What? You don't know Dolores? Ha ha!' and off he went with the pile of sheets in his arms.

'What the hell kind of job does this Palladiani do?' I asked Biancone. 'Any idea?'

Biancone shrugged his shoulders.

A woman came in, one who was still good-looking, despite her haggard, powdered face. 'Ah, are you Dolores?' asked Biancone.

'You kidding?' the woman replied, and went out through another door.

'Okay, then, let's wait.'

After a short while Palladiani came back. He sat between us on the divan, offered us a cigarette, slapped his hand on our knees. 'Ha, ha, my dear friends. Dolores: you'll have a good time.'

'But how much does it cost?' asked Biancone, not letting himself be carried away by that enthusiasm.

'Well, how much did you give to the woman when you

came in? Yes, the one at the entrance . . . What do you mean, nothing? Here you have to pay up front, pay the woman . . .' and he shrugged his shoulders and opened his arms wide, as if to say 'That's the way things work here, nothing you can do about it.'

'Yes, but how much?'

Palladiani, grimacing a bit, mentioned a figure. 'In an envelope, I'd advise you, it's more refined, yes . . .'

'In that case,' replied Biancone, 'let's go immediately, let's pay her at once . . .'

'No, no,' said Palladiani, 'it's not important, you'll pay later . . .'

'Eh, it's better to do it now,' said Biancone, and he was already leading me across the room of card players, then the antechamber, and pushing me down the stairs.

'He's crazy!' he was saying, as we ran down the stairs. 'Out of here, at the double! With Meri-meri we only pay half that.'

Outside in the street we found the little man in the vest.

'Hey, have you been with Pierina?' he asked us. 'Did you say to her: Kneel down?'

'No, we didn't go to her,' we replied, without stopping.

But he was trotting backwards, still standing in front of us, with those round sparkling eyes: 'Kneel down! That's what you say to her: Kneel down! And she, Pierina, kneels down . . .'

We went back to Meri-meri. This time, at our shouts, she came down and opened the door ajar. I had a good look at her: she was tall, thin and horsey, with elongated breasts; she did not look us in the face, she kept her half-shut eyes staring straight in front of her underneath her frizzy hair.

'Come on, let us in,' Biancone was saying to her.

'No, it's late, I'm now going to get some sleep.'

'Oh come on, we've been waiting all night for you.'

'So what? Now I'm tired.'

'We'll only be five minutes, Meri-meri.'

'No, there are two of you, I won't let two of you up together.'

'But just five minutes for each of us . . .'

'In that case,' I said, 'I'll wait . . . Eh? I'll wait outside . . .'

'Okay,' said Biancone, 'I'll come up first then him, is that okay?' To me he said, 'Wait a quarter of an hour for me and I'll come down, then you go up.' He shoved her into the house and went in too.

I took the road towards the sea. I crossed the whole town. A column of armoured cars was going along the main street. At that very moment it came to a halt. In the milky light of their headlamps you could see the soldiers stepping down, stretching their arms and legs, looking around with their sleepy eyes at the dark unknown town.

Immediately there was an order to leave. The drivers went back to the steering wheels, the others clambered up and disappeared into the darkness of their convoys. The column of cars, with their engines roaring, half invisible to eyes blinded by the alternation of light and darkness, moved on and disappeared as though it had never existed.

I reached the harbour. The sea was not sparkling, you could

hear it only by the sound of the waves lapping against the mossy wall of the pier. A slow wave was wearing away at the rocks. In front of the harbour gaol the prison guards walked up and down. I sat down on the jetty, at a point sheltered from the wind. In front of my eyes was the town, with its uncertain lights. I was sleepy and unhappy. The night rejected me. And I was not expecting anything from the day. What was I going to do? I would have liked to lose myself in the night, devote myself body and soul to it, to its darkness, to its revolt, but I realized that what was attractive in it was only a dull, desperate negation of the day. By now not even our local Lupescu attracted me any more: she was a hairy, bony woman, and her house stank. From those houses, those roofs, that mute prison, I would have liked something fermenting in the night to arise, wake up, and open up a different day. 'Only great days,' I thought, 'can have great nights.'

A group of fishermen was approaching the boats tied up to the jetty, carrying oars and nets. They were talking loudly, in that silence. By dawn they would have to be out at sea. They fitted the boats, set off, disappeared into the dark water, and you could still hear their voices in the middle of the sea.

The sense of their wakening in the dark, of their drab early-morning departure, of their rowing in the cold predawn air, doubled the heaviness of my eyes and my shivering. I stretched out my arms as I shivered and yawned. And at that moment, as though it emerged from my chest, the roar of the siren sounded. It was an alarm.

I remembered then about the school, which we had left unguarded, and ran towards the town. These were times when, in our country, we did not yet know what terror was; going through the streets you barely saw the signs of this brusque, general awakening: voices in the houses, blacked-out lights going on and then instantly going out again, and half-dressed people on the threshold of the shelters looking up into the sky.

I got to the school – it was I who had the key – went in, went round the classrooms opening the windows, as I had been instructed. Opening wide one of the windows I heard the buzz: the airplane, both the child and king of that nocturnal world, was crossing the sky laden with bombs. I tried to see it with my eyes, and even more so I tried to imagine the man sitting up there in his cockpit, in the midst of the void, working out his route. It flew past; the sky went back to being deserted and silent again. I went back to our room and sat on the camp bed. As I leafed through the magazine, English cities ripped apart and lit up by tracer bullets went before my eyes. I got undressed and lay down. The siren sounded: the alarm was over.

Shortly afterwards Biancone arrived. He was spruced up, hair combed, chatty, as though the evening was just starting now. He told me how the alarm had ruined his love-making at the crucial point, and described improbable scenes of half-naked women escaping to the shelter. He was seated on his camp bed, I was lying down, and we continued talking for a bit as we smoked. In the end he, too, lay down; we wished each other good morning and sweet dreams; it was dawn.

However, I now could not get to sleep and lay tossing and turning in the bed. At that hour, my father would already have got up, fastened on his leggings, panting as he did so, and slipped on his hunting jacket full of hunting gear. I seemed to hear him moving through the house that was still half asleep and dark, wakening the dog, shushing his barks, talking to him and answering him. He would heat up breakfast on the gas both for himself and the dog; they ate together, in the cold kitchen; then he would sling a big basket over his neck and another one in his hand, and would go out of the house, with long strides, his white goatee beard wrapped in his scarf. Along the mule tracks in the countryside you could almost tell the time from his heavy footfall, accompanied by the dog's jingling collar, and his constant coughing and bringing up catarrh, and those who lived along his route would hear him in their half-asleep state and realize that it was time to get up. With the first light of dawn he would reach his farm, wake the country people up and, before they were at work, he had already gone round all the terraces and examined the work done and still to do, and started to shout and swear, filling the valley with his yells. The older he got, the more his polemical attitude towards the world was crystallized in that early rise of his, in that being the first on his feet in the whole countryside, in that constant rant against everyone – his sons, friends, enemies – that they were a bunch of useless slackers. And maybe his only moments of happiness were these ones at dawn, as he went with his dog along the roads he knew so well, freeing his bronchial tubes of the catarrh that plagued him at night, and watching slowly as the indistinct grey gave way to colours in the rows of vines and between the branches of olive trees, and recognizing the sounds of the early-morning birds one by one.

So, with my thoughts following my father's footsteps through the countryside, I fell asleep; and he never knew that he had had me so close to him.